TROUBLE

Katja Ivar

BITTER LEMON PRESS
LONDON

BITTER LEMON PRESS

First published in the United Kingdom in 2023 by
Bitter Lemon Press, 47 Wilmington Square, London WC1X OET
www.bitterlemonpress.com

A CIP record for this book is available from the British Library

ISBN 978–1–913394–776
EBook ISBN USC 978–1–913394–783
EBook ISBN ROW 978–1–913394–790

Typeset by Tetragon, London

Printed and bound in Great Britain by the
CPI Group (UK) Ltd, Croydon, CRO 4YY

No man means evil but the Devil,
and we shall know him by his horns.

WILLIAM SHAKESPEARE,
The Merry Wives of Windsor, Act V, Scene ii

Prologue

April 1942

The shadows were getting longer. He reckoned that by the time they made it to the train station, night would fall. Ahead of them, the road lay empty. The only thing he could see were the tail lights of a large Volvo truck that had passed them a few minutes ago in a cloud of foul-smelling fumes, slowly, as if looking for something. He wondered if he should ask his family to hurry up, but his wife looked tired after spending all day on her feet. Maybe she had caught Hella's stomach bug too. He thought about his younger daughter, how pale and thin she had looked this morning as she waved them off. Such a contrast to Christina, with her glowing good health and heavy Valkyrie braids. Christina was walking in front of him, pushing Matti's stroller. He tried to wrestle it from her – he was the man of the family, after all – but his daughter laughed him off.

"Back off, Colonel Mauzer," she said, grinning. "You're the one retiring, remember? It's the reason we spent the day visiting this godforsaken place, so you can put your feet up and wait for the fish to bite while you and your pal Kyander talk about the good old days. Shame he couldn't come with you, by the way. It would have been nice for him to see the cabin."

The colonel smiled at his daughter. "Kyander was called into the office at the last minute. You can't hold it against him – it happens more often than you think, in our line of work." Besides, it didn't matter; his mind was already made up. The log house was a gem: just the right size, with a new roof and a porch, and a sauna on the side. Secluded. Lake views. Ridiculously cheap. He had made an offer right there and then, and it had been accepted. Kyander would be happy. The thought made him smile, put a spring in his step. A mile or so left until they reached the station, and then he'd sit on the train and admire his grandson's sleepy face and dream about the future.

"Oh, here it is again," Christina said.

"What?"

"That truck's coming back." She turned to face him, making a show of wrinkling her nose.

He looked. She was right: in the distance he could see the same truck, with its left headlight blinking, charging towards them. It was going fast now. "Move over to the side," he called out to his family. "The road's dry, but you can never be too careful. And it's getting —"

He never finished his sentence. The truck swerved, hitting Matti's stroller first and then, a split second later, Christina. The colonel didn't move, wouldn't have had time to even if he'd wanted to, didn't cry out. He thought briefly of his wife, walking behind him. And of Hella, sick, home alone. Would she find... The truck was upon him now, and in the evening light he locked eyes with the driver. So that was who —

He didn't have the time to finish that thought either. The beast tore right through him, ripping his skin, crushing his bones and what his superiors in Helsinki called "the finest spy mind in all of Europe".

The last thing he heard, as the light dimmed in his eyes, was his wife screaming. And the truck engine revving, speeding away.

1

June 1953

The metal plate on the mantelpiece was covered with a furry grey blanket of dust. Hella picked it up carefully, holding it at arm's length so that she wouldn't sneeze, and ran a damp handkerchief over it. Then she frowned. It was probably the wrong way to clean the makeshift ashtray. Even though some of the dust had adhered to the tissue, the rest stuck to the barbed wire rim in irregular wet clumps. As for the ash at the bottom, it had solidified into a compact mass. Oh well. She didn't smoke anyway. She should probably put it in storage, along with all the other trinkets that crowded the mantelpiece: a pipe, a battered tobacco tin, a pack of cards, a porcelain statuette of a small, snub-nosed shepherd and his shaggy dog.

It had been eleven years, after all. She supposed it was time to move on. Recognize that she'd been lucky, make plans for the future. She could put a vase here instead, or some candles. Something that would make the room look more like a home and less like a shrine to her long-dead family. Instead, she put the ashtray back, next to the little shepherd, and dropped the cloth on the floor, pulling the letter out of her pocket again. Cleaning could wait. She had more important things to do.

> Dear Hella,
>
> I trust you have fully recovered from your injuries.
>
> If you are back in Helsinki, would you come and see me at Headquarters, at your earliest convenience? There's a little matter I would like to discuss with you, which I hope will be of interest. It's in your line of work.

She folded the letter and put it back in her pocket, wondering if Police Chief Jokela had been thinking about the last case he had sent her way. That one certainly hadn't ended well. Maybe Jokela was feeling guilty about what had happened, and that was the reason for this invitation, though Hella doubted it. He was not that type.

> It would be best if you could come by some time after seven in the evening. That way, you would not have to run into too many of your former colleagues. I have alerted them at reception, and they're expecting you.

Hella glanced at her wristwatch. It was almost seven. If she left now, she could be at HQ in forty minutes. And if she walked all the way there and back, maybe that would tire her out and she might finally sleep. As for Jokela's *little matter*, she doubted it would be of interest. *In your line of work*, he had said. To him, she would forever be a *polyssister*, only good for dealing with children or prostitutes, only useful when male police officers could not intervene for reasons of decency. She'd had enough of that. True, her PI business had hit rock bottom after a month-long hospital stay and her recovery in Lapland, but she was determined to make it work. Besides, she thought, with a wary glance at the dust motes already settling back on the mantelpiece, it wasn't like she had any other talents. Nobody in their right mind would hire her for her cooking or cleaning skills, and she could only type with two fingers, so secretarial work was out of the question too.

She put on her straw hat, even though she knew her efforts to look presentable would be lost on Jokela. Picking up her handbag, she opened the front door, stepping out into the evening glow and almost into the arms of a young man she'd never seen before. Dark hair, rueful smile, blue eyes. His hand was raised as if he was about to knock on her door.

"Oh." She squinted up at him. "Hello. Who are you?" She was certain she had never met him before; she would have remembered that smile.

He lowered his hand. "Hi. I'm Erkki Kanerva." The smile grew bigger, dimpling his left cheek but not the right. "Your neighbour." The young man made a vague gesture towards a prim little house that stood next door. "I saw you moving in earlier today, so I thought I'd come and introduce myself. It's good to see someone living here after so long."

Hella ignored the unspoken question, preferring to answer with one of her own. "And what's that?" In his other hand, the man was holding a small rectangular package, clumsily wrapped in kraft paper and secured with string.

"A parcel?" He sounded unsure. "I found it on your doorstep just now." He handed her the package. Hella noticed he was not wearing a wedding ring, though that didn't necessarily mean anything.

"Thank you." Hella half-turned, wondering if she should invite him in, then remembered the tragic failure of her housekeeping efforts and stopped. He could already glimpse part of the living room over her shoulder. She almost expected to see his eyebrows shoot up, but if Erkki Kanerva was shocked by the mess, he was too polite to acknowledge it.

"Thank you for stopping by," she said, dropping the package onto the small side table by the front door. "Now, if you'll excuse me…" She made a show of glancing at her wristwatch. "There's somewhere I need to be."

Erkki Kanerva ran a hand through his hair. "Of course," he said. "But…"

"What?"

That smile again, his eyes on hers. "You haven't told me your name."

"Oh. Hella Mauzer. Hella with an *a*."

"That's a rather unusual name. For a Finn, I mean."

When she'd been young and insecure, she would take the time to explain. She'd say: *My father's family was German, my mother was Estonian, and haven't you heard of Hella Wuolijoki?* But she was beyond caring what anyone thought of her, and at twenty-nine she wasn't all that young either. In fact, she was probably a couple of years older than the good-looking boy on her doorstep.

She raised her eyebrows. "Is that so? It was very nice to meet you, Mr Kanerva. You'll probably notice that I tend to keep to myself, so it seems unlikely we'll meet again. Have a good evening."

"And you too, Miss Mauzer. It was a pleasure." Smiling, he doffed an imaginary cap to her, then took a step back from her porch. Now his blue eyes were level with hers. "I certainly hope you're wrong, and that we do meet again."

2

The clock on the dome of Helsinki Cathedral was striking eight when Hella stopped in front of the three-storey yellow building on Aleksanterinkatu. She lifted her gaze towards the windows, catching the glint of the evening sun on the glass. A lifetime ago, she'd spent a few years working in that building, running up and down its creaky steps, trying to be one of the boys. Leaving it was heartbreaking, but now she didn't miss it one bit. Too much of an old boys' club for her, and too stifling in the winter, when the windows were sealed tight against the assault of the freezing wind blowing off the sea and the gas fires hissed like a bag of serpents.

When he had become police chief a few months earlier, Jokela surprised everyone but Hella by keeping his old office. Generous souls whispered that it was because he wanted to stay close to his troops, or was too modest for the grand locale vacated by the retiring Dr Palmu. Hella, who had never thought of herself as a generous soul, suspected the reason lay elsewhere. Jokela was like an old predator. He knew his own limitations and sagely preferred to keep to familiar hunting grounds.

The bored young recruit behind the reception desk

nodded when he heard her name. "Yes, the boss's still here. He's working late. Third floor to the left —"

"I know the way."

As Hella climbed the stairs, she wondered whether Jokela would be drunk. She hadn't seen him since the incident that the police and press had qualified as an unfortunate accident. While she'd lain in a narrow hospital bed fighting for her life, he'd brought her flowers, yellow tulips that, at that time of the year, must have cost him a small fortune. Sometimes, in her dreams, those tulips still haunted her. But what had happened to her had not been Jokela's fault, or not entirely his fault. Maybe the unfortunate "accident", and everything that had ensued, haunted him too.

"There you are! My dear girl!" Jokela beckoned her into his office. Definitely drunk, and not just because he was slurring. She could smell a malty tang of whisky in the air that he had tried to mask by spraying cologne. "How have you been? Take a seat, take a seat. You look good, by the way, have you put on weight?" Hella slumped into the visitor's chair. It was so like her old boss to comment on her physical appearance.

She glanced at Jokela, wondering if she should return the compliment, but there was no way she could tell him he looked good. If anything, he looked purple, the spider's web of ruptured veins on his face matching the dull stone in the pin on his tie. "I'm fine," she said. "I got your letter."

Jokela cackled. "Straight to the point, I see. Haven't changed one bit. Not that I'm surprised, not really. Never thought people did change. In my view, they just grow more like themselves as they get older. Well, about the letter." He sighed, dropping the smile. His beefy face grew long, and almost sad. "You see, we've been busy around here,

16

working our socks off to establish a modern police force. Traffic, forensics, organized crime – the works. Lots of new people joining the force. Some leaving, too."

Hella nodded. She still couldn't see what he was getting at. Surely he wasn't planning to propose she rejoin the homicide squad? Would she even consider accepting it if he did?

Jokela's hairy fingers had seized on a matchbook and were snapping it open and shut. "And this, ahem, is the reason I wrote to you." He cleared his throat. "We've known each other for what, ten years now?"

"Eight."

"That's right. Eight. And before I met you, I knew your father. You're a bright girl, and you can be trusted."

Well, this is new, Hella thought. But would he ever get to the point? She looked out of the window at the shiny white mass of the cathedral basking in the sun. When days dragged on forever, people lost all notion of time. "So, what was it you wanted to see me about?"

Jokela looked away. "Well, there's a man we'd like to hire, to fill my old position as head of the homicide squad. We considered Pinchus first, but he's a practising Jew. He even spent time in a labour camp during the war. I don't know if you're aware of this, but the SUPO parked a number of Jews out of sight for a few years before releasing them into society again. So in the end, I decided that it wouldn't do…" His voice trailed off. Hella waited. "So, this candidate we have in mind," Jokela said, giving the matchbook a vigorous squeeze, "is a most distinguished man. As a matter of fact, he currently works for the SUPO."

Of course, Hella thought. A secret service man. Probably knows nothing about policing or detective work, but who did that ever stop when deciding on a promotion?

"His name is Johannes Heikkinen," her former boss added, as if an afterthought. "I'd like you to do a background check on him." Jokela set down the matchbook and looked her in the eye.

"I'm sorry," Hella said. "I still don't see where I come in. Surely if your candidate worked for the SUPO, you have all the information you need?"

Now it was Jokela's turn to contemplate the cathedral across the square. "We do. We do and we don't. We have the dates, and the performance appraisals, a list of his skills and the languages he speaks, but that's all." He turned to face her. "I'd like to know more than that. I need to know what he's *like*."

Hella reached for her handbag and stood up to leave. "I'm sorry, Jon. But you're not being frank with me, and I feel like I'm wasting my time here. I can't work if you don't tell me what you suspect him of."

"Nothing. Absolutely nothing." Jokela rubbed his face with both hands. "Just thought that you might like a nice easy job, a bit of pocket money. I mean, I owe you an easy job this time around, right?"

"Thank you, Jon, but last I heard, free cheese was only available in mousetraps." Hella shook her head and turned for the door. "I hope the candidate will prove to be suitable for the job."

"Wait. Close the door. Sit down. You're right, there is something."

She took a seat again and waited.

"The job is confidential. SUPO wouldn't be happy to learn that we're looking into one of their own. That's one of the reasons I called you – the other being that I couldn't very well ask one of my own men to investigate his future boss." Jokela lowered his voice, and she had to lean forward not to miss anything. The whisky smell was getting stronger. "And it's probably nothing. It's just that we can't take the risk. *I* can't."

"What risk?"

Jokela continued as if he hadn't heard. "They say it runs in families. And they're probably right. Mr Heikkinen's father committed suicide – it's in his son's personnel file – and apparently his cousin is off his rocker, and then his child and wife died and he went off on a bit of a tangent himself."

"I see," Hella said.

"Of course you do." Jokela visibly perked up. "So I'd like you to make sure the man doesn't have… issues, I suppose that's what you'd call it. You know, that he doesn't bark with the dogs, or secretly believe he's the Messiah or something. What with your female intuition, you have an eye for such things."

Hella bit her lip, thinking. It made sense. Jokela was walking on eggshells in his new position, and he couldn't afford to bring in someone who might be unstable. Well, maybe free cheese existed after all, because this was exactly the sort of boring job that paid well. And, besides, she had an idea that might even make the assignment worthwhile.

"All right," she said. "I'll do it. But —"

"Splendid! Wonderful!" Jokela fished a sheet of paper out of his desk drawer and slid it towards her. "Here are his details and the addresses of some of the people who know him. Go and speak to them. Take your time. I'm off shooting crows in Nuuksio tomorrow, so you do what you need to do, and we can talk about it at the end of the week."

"But," Hella said, "in return, I want access to the police archives. I'd like to see what's in my family's file." She held her breath.

To her relief, Jokela waved an impatient hand. "If you wish. Not a problem for me. I'll leave word with whoever's in charge."

"Thank you." She took the sheet of paper and, folding it in two, slid it into her handbag. "I'll get started tomorrow."

She decided it wasn't necessary to tell him that she would be starting with the archives. There must be something, some trail she could pick up, to find who had been driving the truck that killed her family. Maybe that would make moving back into her childhood home a little easier.

3

When she turned her key in the lock, it was already past ten, but the sunshine streaming through the dirty windows was still mercilessly picking out the old worn-out furniture, the stacks of books on the floor and the pendant light wrapped in a mosquito net. Hella dropped her keys on the side table, and that was when she noticed the package she received earlier in the day. No name on it, and no return address. Was it even for her? The paper wrapping felt grimy, as if someone had been carrying it around for weeks, and prudence dictated that she throw it away without opening it. Unfortunately, prudence had never been one of Hella's defining qualities, so she took the package with her as she went into the kitchen to make coffee.

The kitchen still looked as if its rightful owners had only stepped out for a second. Her mother's check apron lay folded on the counter, the bread box was gaping open, and there was a mummified something in a little glass by the window. Upon closer inspection it turned out to be the remains of a spring onion. Hella unscrewed the lid on a tin of coffee and grabbed a small copper pot from a box that contained the few belongings she had brought over with her. The water, when she turned on the tap, ran rusty, and she had to wait for a few minutes until it lost that orange hue. Then she lit a match, half expecting the fire not to take, but it did.

While she waited for the coffee to boil, she forced herself to stare out of the window, at the cute wooden house that her cute new neighbour with his cute smile lived in. Anything but face the calendar on the wall, with its jumble of black dates and pen marks crawling around like insects. April the sixteenth, the date her parents and sister and Matti had gone to visit the cabin, was circled. She had seen them off and then stumbled back into bed, nauseous and weak, her head swimming. She had spent that day drifting in and out of sleep and running to the basin to throw up, feeling sorry for herself because no one was around to hold her hair or bring her a glass of water. And then, when dusk had already set in and she was starting to wonder what was taking them so long, there had been a knock on the door...

Hella gritted her teeth. The coffee was boiling now, and she poured herself a cup and carried it into the living room before returning to the kitchen to grab the strange parcel and a pair of scissors.

The string gave way easily. Hella put it aside and slowly unwrapped the paper. She did not know what to expect: a welcome gift, maybe, prepared by some myopic neighbourhood granny, or a personal garment she might have forgotten at the hospital, or even a dead rat. What fell out of the wrapping made no sense at all, though. A handkerchief-sized piece of grey felt tissue, well-worn, stained and shiny in places. And a slip of paper with some numbers on it: *169062*. She supposed the sender must have hoped the contents of the parcel would mean something to her. Hella peered at the paper, turning it in her hand. Maybe this was meant for someone else and had been dropped on her doorstep by mistake? Or maybe it was some sort of joke? She carefully wrapped the parcel again and put it on the coffee table – it seemed oddly at home among the mess that was her living room – then took a sip of her coffee. She had forgotten to pick up food, and now it was too late to go out, but that was all right, because she wasn't hungry. Maybe it was the prospect of sleeping in her childhood room, with the rose-buds blooming on the faded wallpaper and a photograph of a smiling Christina and Matti tucked under the mirror's frame. Or maybe it was the loneliness. She had told only a few people that she was moving back to her parents' house, because she still wasn't sure it was the right decision. Even so, someone must have known.

She squinted down at the parcel on her coffee table, then got up. No one was watching her; it was just her imagina-tion. Still, she walked to the window and pulled the curtains closer together. A midnight sun was seeping through the fabric, a light that even the tightly drawn curtains could not extinguish. The room was bathed in milky dusk, and suddenly she knew with absolute certainty that she wouldn't be able to sleep. But what else could she do? She filled her coffee cup to the brim, then made her way upstairs, towards the cosy little room with its faded rosebuds and its narrow metal-framed bed.

4

The pale dusk of the night slipped on the bright colours of day as Hella was brushing her teeth above the bathroom sink. There was no sunrise any more, the sun never properly set. Instead, it hovered for hours above the horizon, as if making up its mind, before briefly dipping out of sight then reappearing on the other side of the sky in a conjuring trick. How was anyone supposed to sleep if it was never dark? How was anyone supposed to *think*?

She spat out the toothpaste and inspected her face in the broken mirror. She had no memory of it, but she must have smashed it herself after learning that she was an orphan; there was a fine scar running along the palm of her right hand and she could remember sitting in some windowless white room while a doctor pulled out shards of glass and chided her for her carelessness. Now her reflection in the mirror looked strangely satisfying, like a catalogue of spare parts for a woman's face: a high forehead framed by dark sweeps of hair. Grey eyes. The sharp line of a jawbone, the skin pale and smooth. A large mouth. Hella picked up a towel to wipe her face, before pulling her hair up and twisting it into a bun that to all intents and purposes resembled a cowpat. Then she made her way downstairs.

She avoided looking at the parcel on her way out of the house, but she did cast an inquiring glance towards the house next door. No one. Just as well. She had no time to waste making chit-chat with neighbours; there was work to be done.

On her way to Headquarters, Hella stopped in the market square, where she bought a *korvapuusti*. She ate the cinnamon bun sitting on a bench in the harbour, next to the Cholera Basin. The air was chilly and she congratulated herself on her choice of clothes, which included a long-sleeved jacket. People tended to forget when the sun was shining, but Helsinki is a port city, and the weather usually stays in the teens, even in the summer. As she ate, she tried to imagine what this part of the city had looked like a hundred years before, when it was still the muddy Kaupunginlahti bay and rats as big as badgers infested the harbour. Now elegantly dressed ladies in hug-me-tights and patent leather shoes hurried around on uneven cobblestones and the Cholera Basin was just a name, not a mortal danger.

With the last of the *korvapuusti* gone, Hella brushed the crumbs off her skirt and hurried up Helenankatu before turning left, towards the vast expanse of Senate Square and the neoclassical splendour of Helsinki Cathedral. Here, too, things had changed in the past hundred years, and almost no one cared to remember that the cathedral had initially been built as a tribute to the Grand Duke of Finland, who was also Tsar Nicholas I of Russia. Now the Soviet Union was neither a master nor a friend but more like a menacing presence on their doorstep. And at the same time… things were changing there too. Stalin, who everyone had expected would live forever, was dead, and his successors were starting to embark on a series of reforms. Hella glanced at the *Helsingin Sanomat* headlines in the newspaper kiosk as she passed it by: HUNDREDS OF POLITICAL PRISONERS FREED FROM SOVIET LABOUR CAMPS. An emaciated man's face was pictured under the caption, eyes wild with hope, a toothless grin. And, behind him, a long line of convicts. Hella shivered and pushed open the door to the police headquarters.

The archives occupied a long dusty room at the back of the building. In all her years on the force, Hella had only been there twice, the first time on the day of her arrival when she had sneaked in to ask if there was a file on Colonel and Mrs Mauzer. At that time, the answer was no – they had told her that because the hit-and-run was still being investigated by the local police force, it had not been escalated to Headquarters. The answer was still no when she went down to inquire a year later. But a lot of time had passed since then. There was a chance the file was there now.

"What can I do for you?"

Hella turned. She knew that her old colleague Ranta had retired earlier that year, so she had been expecting to meet the new officer in charge of the archives. What she didn't expect was that he'd look so forbidding: six foot six and three feet wide, his shirt straining against a beer belly, a face like a potato on which someone had stuck a pair of tiny, cornflower-blue eyes. "My name's Mauzer," she said. "Chief Jokela must have —"

"I know who you are," grumbled the man. He was looking down at her with undisguised hostility. "What do you want to look at?"

"Two things." Hella checked her notes. Heikkinen's mad cousin was named Veikko Aalto. "I'd like to know if you have anything on this man," she said. She glanced towards the floor-to-ceiling metal shelves stacked loosely with cardboard files. Helsinki was a small city and criminality levels were low. Checking the archives shouldn't take too long.

The officer folded his beefy arms. "You said there were two things."

"Yes. The other file I want to consult concerns the deaths of Colonel and Mrs Mauzer, their daughter Christina, and their grandson Matti on 16 April 1942. They died in a hit-and-run accident."

"All right, stay here." The man pointed to a rickety chair by the door, then bent low over a leather-bound ledger. "Here it is. Don't move, I'll bring you the files." He was gone for less than two minutes before he returned, a nasty smile on his face. He was carrying two files. "I can't let you take them out, but you can read them all you like here. Nothing serious for Aalto. Drunken brawls. Petty mischief. Annoying his neighbours, that kind of thing. No criminal record, just a few warnings." The officer was looming above her, offering a view of a triple chin and, above it, nose hair. "Anything else, Miss?"

"No thank you. Just give me the files."

Because he was watching her, she started with Veikko Aalto's file. Nothing serious, the officer had said. Hella wasn't so sure. Apart from a few complaints made by his next-door neighbour (for which no details were provided), there were two calls to the police made by Johannes Heikkinen. Here, too, there were no further details. Only the date and time of call, and a note that the complainant had later informed the police that the issue had been resolved. A family feud? A drunken brawl? Whatever it was, it must have been serious enough for a trained SUPO officer to call the cops. Still, she couldn't very well ask Heikkinen what it was about. The year on the complaints was 1948. She opened her notebook and jotted down the name of the neighbour: Mr Sopanen.

Then, her heart racing, she set the Aalto file aside and picked up the one titled *Colonel Mauzer and Family*. The cardboard was scuffed in places, the ink barely visible. There was a stain left by a coffee cup in the upper right-hand corner. She looked up. The officer was smirking, a look of eager anticipation on his potato face.

"Take your time, Miss."

Hella already knew what to expect, but she opened the file anyway. It was empty.

"Thank you," she said, getting up. "You've been very helpful. If it's all right with you, I might come back later."

If the man picked up on the sarcasm, it didn't show. "I thought you might. Any time you like." There was barely controlled aggression behind his mask of jovial good humour.

When Jokela was back from shooting crows, Hella thought as she trudged back towards reception, she'd ask him to personally go down to the archives and inquire about the file. Provided, of course, that she'd have something to show him at the end of her investigation. Not for the first time, she wondered why Jokela had hired her. Was it, like the police chief had told her, because he wanted to make sure the candidate represented no danger to his reputation? Or did he know there would be something to find, and that this something would give him power over the new head of the homicide squad? And would she ever know which of these it was?

Deep in thought, Hella retraced her steps back to the harbour, and from there to Katajanokka. Heikkinen lived on Kruunuvuorenkatu, not that far, she realized, from the yellow art nouveau house occupied by her father's old friend and colleague, Kyander. The island's architecture dated back mainly to the turn of the century, when graceful pastel-coloured apartment buildings had sprung up on the western part known as the "old side". Now, there were only a few individual homes left, stuck awkwardly between bigger houses. As she walked, she wondered if Kyander still lived there. Or had he finally bought himself a cabin by the lake for his retirement (if people in his line of work ever actually retired)? And what was it with these old spies – did they all need to live close to the military fort and the county prison? But she had to admit that Katajanokka had its charms, not least the breathtaking sea views and the marvellous imagination of the architects who had designed the houses. Heikkinen's apartment building was painted yellow too. It boasted whiplash curves, sloping arches and graceful balcony railings. Hella passed it by with merely a sideways glance. She was planning to speak to the man, but not yet. In the best tradition of sleuthing, she decided to start her investigation by interviewing the neighbours.

5

"So," Steve said. He rose, unsmiling, when he saw her. "Here you are."

She had found him sitting on her doorstep when she got back from Katajanokka. She could tell he'd been waiting for a while; he was hunched over, and the newspaper next to him lay folded in on itself, the crossword puzzle on the last page filled out in blue ink.

"Here I am." She pushed past him, unlocking the door.

Sighing, Steve picked up his paper and followed her inside. "You could have told me you were moving. I would have helped with your things."

She looked at him with narrowed eyes. "Steve, you and I are *over*, remember? I assumed we'd agreed on that."

"You didn't leave me much choice, did you?"

He dropped into a chair, stretching his long legs under the coffee table. She hadn't opened the curtains yet, but even in the muted light his hair gleamed gold. Hella thought, as she often did, that the years had been good to him. Steve did not look a day over thirty – and a handsome thirty at that.

"By the way," he said, "a man came to see you."

"What man?"

"He said he lived next door. Erkki something."

The way he said it made Hella turn away to hide a smile. "Did he mention what he wanted?"

"Not to me." Steve locked his fingers behind his head. "So, what have you been up to? If I'm not mistaken, that's your professional outfit."

The only decent one, Hella thought. Though hardly becoming, or comfortable. She hadn't worn it in months, and now the skirt was too tight.

"Jokela offered me a job," she said.

"That old bastard?" Steve raised an eyebrow. "Last time he sent a client your way, you almost died."

"It's a different sort of job. A boring routine sort of job." Hella shrugged. "He wants me to check out a prospective recruit, see if I can find any skeletons in his closet."

"And have you found any?"

Hella thought about Heikkinen's dead child, and his dead wife. "Not so far, but I'm just getting started. I chatted to his greengrocer today, and to the guy who sweeps the street: both say he's nice and quiet, and always polite."

"Exactly the kind of men that invariably turn out to be ruthless killers, if your past experience is anything to go by. I'd be careful if I were you." Steve was leaning forward, his gaze on the parcel. "What's that?"

"I don't know. It was left on my doorstep last night. Must be some mistake."

She had tried to make her voice sound light, but Steve was no fool. He squinted up at her. "And what's inside?"

"Just tissue." She shrugged. "And a piece of paper with some numbers. And before you ask, the numbers mean nothing to me."

"I don't suppose it's a code for a treasure hunt?" Steve's brow creased in concern. "Is that why you keep your curtains drawn? Do you think someone might be watching you?"

"Absolutely not!" Scowling, Hella marched towards the window and pulled the curtains wide open. "There. Feel better?"

The light did nothing to improve the appearance of the room, but that was now the least of her worries. Steve put the parcel back on the table. "You think it could be that man next door?"

Hella blinked irritably against the sun streaming in through the window. "Could it be him what?"

"The one who left you this parcel. Your neighbour seems a total creep, in case you haven't noticed."

"You're sick, Steve Collins." She glanced at her wrist-watch. "Aren't you going to be late for the broadcast?"

He was still looking at her. "You're right. But I was hoping to talk about where we stand, you and I. You've barely spoken to me since the accident, and I need to know."

Need to know what? Hella thought. She wanted to scream. *I waited for you for five years, and I'm tired of waiting. You made it perfectly clear that I'll always come second after your wife.* She must have said that last sentence out loud, because Steve frowned. "Ex-wife. Elsbeth and I divorced. Last month. Just like I said we would." He rose. "Seriously, Hella, we need to talk. Maybe not now, but soon. I miss you."

"I don't." She walked towards the door and held it open for him.

"You would test a saint's patience, you know that?" Steve's face was serious, but his eyes were smiling. "Must be why I love you."

"Goodbye, Steve." She bolted the door when he left then leaned against it, suddenly drained of all energy, and closed her eyes. What was wrong with her? Ever since the accident, she hadn't been herself: she couldn't focus, couldn't think clearly. Or was it this house? Had she made a mistake, moving back here? She opened her eyes, and her gaze found the coffee table, and the strange parcel. It looked as innocent as a landmine that no one had stepped on yet.

6

Hella spent the rest of the afternoon going through her notes. Apart from the greengrocer, and the street-sweeper, she had also managed to talk to Heikkinen's next-door neighbour, a pop-eyed woman of indeterminate age dressed in a furry gilet, as if in defiance of the summer heat. Much to Hella's surprise and delight, the woman had waved her in as soon as she had opened her front door. "It's up there," she said, pointing. "I hope you don't mind the stairs."

"Not at all," Hella had replied, puzzled. She had prepared a story about looking for a long-lost friend of her older brother, but apparently no such story was needed. She started making her way up the stairs, heard the pop-eyed woman labouring in her wake. "Which way?"

"Left."

Left of the landing was a tidy little room containing a single bed covered with a pristine white bedspread, a mahogany chest of drawers and a chair that was used as a nightstand.

"Do you smoke?" the woman puffed.

"No." So this woman had a room to let! Hella congratulated herself on wearing her only skirt suit, which made her look like a secretary or a lowly office worker, a decent, hard-working girl, and, as her ringless finger proved, a spinster. "Is it noisy?" she asked, because that was the sort of thing a spinster would ask. "I'm a light sleeper, can't stand it when people argue next door."

"The gentleman next door is very quiet," the woman said in an uncertain voice. "And he lives alone."

"Does he drink?" She was probably overdoing it, but she had a feeling the woman was holding something back. "Because sometimes when people drink, even if they're usually quiet —"

"I've never seen Mr Heikkinen drunk," the woman said. "Any lady visitors?"

"None at all." The owner frowned. "Don't you want to check the bed, or see the bathroom?"

Hella dutifully sat on the bed and bounced, testing the springs. It was a shame she had to disturb such a perfect arrangement, but she needed time to think. She couldn't ask about Mr Heikkinen's crazy cousin, or his dead wife and child. Unfortunately, her mind was as blank as the bare walls of the room. And then, as she was preparing to rise and retreat, she heard it. Lively tempo, triple metre, a strong accent on the second beat. A mazurka? Hella strained to listen. "Is that your neighbour playing? Sounds like Chopin."

"Mr Heikkinen never plays during the night," the pop-eyed woman protested. "Or early in the morning. And the walls of his house are exceptionally thick. It's been built to last."

"But I bet he plays in the evening, doesn't he?" Hella rose from the bed. "I'm afraid I won't need to see the bathroom. I'm looking for a place where I'm sure to get my beauty sleep."

Now, back in her parents' living room, sitting on the sofa, she yawned, thinking that as long as she got *any* sleep, she'd be fine. Maybe she should try to go to bed earlier. She even glanced at her wristwatch, but it was only six, and it seemed silly to go to bed this early. She hadn't even had her dinner yet.

She looked at her notes again. By all accounts, Johannes Heikkinen was a model citizen. Turning to a fresh page in her notebook, she wrote down the epithets that people she had met earlier in the day had used to describe the man.

Quiet.

Calm.

Charitable.

Polite.

Prompt.

Kindly.

Hella rubbed her nose with the tip of her pencil, then added in her own observation: *A good pianist.*

Now what? No one she had talked to had said *mad*. No one had said *angry*. Or even *unkind*.

Come to think of it, the only curious thing that had come up so far was the absence of any strangeness that could prompt an investigation. A spy's way of hiding things? Act as ordinary as it gets, to make sure no one will come looking?

And did she have to second-guess everything? Hella sighed and closed her notebook. Tomorrow, she'd try to find out how Heikkinen's wife and child had died, because Jokela's file was vague about that. Then, she'd interview the crazy cousin. In the meantime, she needed to go and buy some food. Coffee was all well and good, but a girl couldn't live on coffee alone. She needed eggs. And bread. And some carrots, and potatoes and –

There was a knock on her door. Hella didn't move. It could be Steve coming back, but she didn't want to see him. Or anyone else, for that matter. What she wanted was something to eat, preferably full of butter and sugar, and then to crawl into bed and forget about the blinding sun. What she needed —

There was another knock, louder this time. Stifling a curse, Hella rose and smoothed her skirt. Her dark hair had escaped from her bun, and she shook out the rest of the pins as she went to open the door. It was not Steve. Instead, her new neighbour stood on her doorstep and, like the last time, he was smiling.

"What?"

"Good evening, Miss Mauzer. I hope I'm not interrupting…"

Hella glanced over her shoulder, looking at the lonely little room. "Not at all."

"I was hoping that…" His cheeks coloured slightly. "I was wondering if…"

She waited.

"I was wondering if you'd like to go out to dinner with me."

7

Lying in her childhood bed, the patchwork quilt pulled up to her nose, Hella watched the sky change from grey to pink to gold. She had managed to snatch a couple of hours' fitful sleep between two and four – nowhere near enough to feel rested. She'd never thought she'd miss the endless polar night of Lapland, but she did. She had told Erkki as much, over what turned out to be a delightful dinner at a tiny restaurant by the water. When they arrived, the red wooden hut was packed with locals like a fish kettle, so they chose to sit outside, looking out at the sea. They ate grilled sausages and blueberry pie washed down with coffee. Perhaps because he was a good judge of character, Erkki didn't ask her any questions, not at first. Instead, he talked to her about his work as a mechanical engineer at Sisu, and about the renovations he had embarked on in his little house. Sanding floorboards, replacing electrical fixtures, installing a new sink in the kitchen and wall-mounted cabinets for the glassware. "A fully equipped kitchen," he exclaimed, smiling. "What a bachelor like me is going to do with it once it's finished, I have no idea! I don't even know how to grill a steak."

Hella bit into her bread to avoid answering, and looked away at the little boats bobbing on the waves. As she often did, she thought about her sister. Christina would have offered to teach her cute neighbour how to cook and she would have looked adorable doing it. She'd have known exactly what to say and do. And then another thought hit her. Was he coming on to her? Did all this talk about his home-improvement skills and being a bachelor mean anything?

"I wouldn't know how to grill a steak if my life depended on it," she said, still looking at the boats.

Erkki laughed. He had a good laugh, the kind that made you want to join in, and Hella found herself smiling. "I'm not exaggerating," she said. "I have no homemaking skills whatsoever. When I lived in Lapland, I had a landlady who liked to cook. I thought I might learn from her, but somehow I never did."

"What did you do in Lapland?" Erkki picked up the coffee pot and refilled her cup.

"I was a police officer. In Ivalo. What?"

He was looking at her with his head cocked to the side, as if his beliefs were being put to the test.

"No, really," she said, feeling foolish. She considered adding that, before Ivalo, she had been a member of the Helsinki homicide squad, then decided against it.

Erkki was still looking at her. Then he laughed. "Now that's a surprise. Are you still with the police?"

Hella shook her head. "No, not any more. I left the force last year" – *was fired from the force* would probably be more accurate, but somehow she didn't feel like saying that – "and then I started working as a PI. Here, in Helsinki. You can't work as a PI in Ivalo. It doesn't make sense, unless you specialize in looking for lost reindeer. Even here, work is hard to come by."

"Is that why you moved into your parents' house?"

She was instantly on her guard. What had Steve said? "Could your neighbour be the one spying on you?" A ridiculous thought, of course, but one she couldn't shake off easily. "How do you know it's my parents' house?"

"Because of the name. When I moved into my place, I was told the house belonged to Mr and Mrs Mauzer, and I haven't seen any men around. Except for the tall gentleman who stopped by earlier today." He looked at her inquiringly.

"No." Hella laughed, shaking her head. "There's no Mr Mauzer. Just me. And the reason I moved here was because I had a bad accident last spring. When I was out of hospital, I went to stay with friends in Lapland for a while, and I thought I'd be fine, but when I got back to Helsinki, I found I was struggling to climb the stairs to my fourth-floor apartment." There was also the fact that money was tight, although he didn't need to know *that*.

"What sort of accident?" Erkki asked.

What could she tell him? *I was chased by a serial killer, fell through the ice and almost drowned?* It sounded rather melodramatic. The last thing she wanted was for Erkki to think of her as some helpless little thing, a police officer not up to her job. Or, worse, feel sorry for her. "Just a stupid accident," she said. "I wasn't careful enough."

He opened his mouth, probably to ask for more details, then thought better of it. "Well, I'm glad you're here now." He pushed the untouched blueberry pie on his plate towards her. "You look like you could do with another serving."

"Oh no," she laughed. She realized she'd been laughing a lot, and not always at the right times. If she was being honest with herself, the correct word to describe the noises she was making was *giggling*. Like a schoolgirl. Maybe it was the lack of sleep, or the fairy-tale glimmer of the midnight sun. Almost without thinking, she picked up the spoon and started on Erkki's blueberry pie. The waiter was going round the tables, lighting candles stuck in Kilner jars. A silver-haired couple at the table next to them were talking in low voices, a soft smile on the woman's lined but still beautiful face. "Yeah, I'm glad I'm here too." Now that the pie plate was empty, Hella put her spoon down. "I wasn't too sure at first, but now I'm glad I'm here."

8

The morning sun was steadily climbing into the inevitable blue sky when Hella locked the front door behind her. She paused on the porch, glancing over at Erkki's house. His curtains were still drawn, the front door closed. Hella surveyed the rest of the street, on the lookout for anything unusual. She still couldn't get rid of the feeling of being watched.

There was a van she'd never seen before, parked on the kerb a few feet from her doorstep. Its side bore an inscription in ten-inch-tall letters: SAVE AND PROTECT, with the image of a guard dog and an address in Ruskeasuo underneath. Passing in front of it, Hella looked through the driver's window: empty. It probably didn't mean anything, but she was still feeling unnerved by the strange parcel. That morning, abandoning her smart suit, Hella had opted instead for a yellow polka-dot dress and a cardigan. She was hoping for a cosy, intimate conversation, and a smart suit wouldn't do for that. As she had lain awake the previous night, she tried to list her options: approaching Heikkinen directly seemed out of the question, so she decided she'd start with those who knew him best and were most likely to talk. His dead wife's sister was at the top of the list, and Hella was hoping to find her at home.

Mrs Liisa Vanhanen, small, bird-boned, her platinum hair in a poodle cut, opened the door almost before Hella had time to knock. She must have been expecting someone else, though, because immediately her mouth rounded into a little *o* of surprise. Facing a pair of suspicious and unwelcoming eyes, Hella had no choice but to lie.

"I'm from the SUPO." She smiled brightly, extending a hand for Mrs Vanhanen to shake.

"From the SUPO?" Now the eyes were round too. Over the woman's shoulder, Hella could see the hall, decked out in flowered wallpaper, and, beyond, a door open on the living room, where a small table was set for coffee.

Hella lowered her voice to a confidential whisper. "How about we step inside? In case your neighbours get curious?"

"Of course, of course," the woman said, flustered, leading Hella towards the living room. The hall, small and spotlessly clean, smelled of wood polish. "This is so unexpected. I thought you were my mother."

Hella smiled without answering. Her cover story, which she had cobbled together as she walked, was simple enough. Mr Heikkinen was up for a major promotion. There were procedures that had to be followed. But this wasn't terribly important, just a formality, so his supervisors hadn't bothered sending a man to do the background interviews. A secretary was enough. She was that secretary.

The woman was still talking, her face a mixture of curiosity and apprehension. "You see, my mother comes round for a morning coffee every Tuesday… I've just cut the cake." She gestured towards the table, as if Hella required proof of what she was saying. There, surrounded by a coffee pot, a milk jug and two small saucers containing jam, stood a large Åland pancake. A thrifty housewife's dish: Hella's mother used to make these too, out of semolina or rice pudding, whatever was available. Now Hella thought about it, the rest of the room also looked like a place where her mother would have felt at home: inexpensive yet welcoming, with cushions scattered on the sofa, well-ironed curtains framing sparkling windows, and trinkets on the mantelpiece without a speck of dust on them. Hella was almost tempted to ask Mrs Vanhanen for advice on house cleaning, but one look at the woman's worried face and she remembered why she was there.

"Is this... what is this about?" the woman mumbled. "Isn't the SUPO concerned with national security?" She held her breath.

"Oh. No. Well, yes, but not just national security. I need to speak to you about your brother-in-law, Johannes Heikkinen. If you have a moment."

"What's happened?" The mention of Heikkinen's name seemed to throw the woman into even greater confusion. She opened her mouth to speak, closed it again. Sitting down, she motioned for Hella to do the same. "I haven't seen him since Easter."

"Nothing's happened. At least, as far as I know. Just a standard background check."

It was surprising to see what a simple mention of the SUPO could do. Mrs Vanhanen's hands were shaking. Hella watched as the woman cut generous slices of pancake for them both. She wondered if she hadn't overdone it, and smiled to reassure her hostess. "He's up for a promotion, and this is a routine check. Which is why Mr Heikkinen's employers, who have better things to do, entrusted me with this task." She smiled self-deprecatingly. "I'm a secretary, you see. But you must promise not to say a word about this to him. This is confidential."

"Of course. Stewed prunes or blueberry jam? Help yourself." The woman was serving coffee now, pouring it to the brim.

"Stewed prunes," Hella said. "Thank you." She bit into the cake. Semolina. Her favourite. "So, what sort of a man is Mr Heikkinen? You must know him well."

"A wonderful man! The best there is. Decent, kind, generous to a fault."

"I see," Hella said, narrowing her eyes at this display of unchecked enthusiasm. "I'm sorry to bring up sad memories, but I understand your sister and her child passed away?"

"Yes. But not at the same time." The woman took a sip of her coffee. "That poor baby only lived a day, they didn't even have time to name him. A weak heart, the doctor said. Maria died two years after that, to the day. But that was a long time ago. It'll be five years in September."

"What happened?" Hella wondered how to explain the reason for her question, should the woman challenge it, but Mrs Vanhanen, having accepted the principle of a SUPO secretary making inquiries, expressed no further reservations. Or maybe she was just happy to talk.

"There was a fire at their house. Johannes was working late, but he arrived shortly after it broke out. He was badly burned trying to save Maria, but it was too late. He pulled her out, but she had already suffocated from the fumes, that's what the doctor said."

"Oh." Hella wondered if she should ask how the fire started, but she couldn't pretend that a question like that might be part of her basic investigation. "I'm so sorry. I imagine Mr Heikkinen must have been heartbroken."

"Worse than that." Her hostess brought out a small lacy handkerchief and delicately blew her nose, before folding it again and pushing it up her sleeve. "Everyone thought he wouldn't survive either. He became a ghost of a man. Wouldn't eat, wouldn't sleep. We thought it best that he move house, but he wanted to keep living in that place. He said he felt closer to Maria there."

"He never remarried?"

Mrs Vanhanen shook her poodle curls. "No. My mother tried to bring it up once. She told him that would be only natural. He said the idea hadn't even crossed his mind. That Maria was the only woman he had ever loved, and her death wasn't reason enough to be unfaithful. He still keeps her slippers by her side of the bed, you know. And her bottle of perfume – lily of the valley – in the bathroom. He just can't forget her."

Hella nodded sympathetically, marvelling at this paragon of virtue. "Does Mr Heikkinen have any flaws?"

"No," the woman said. She was about to add something else, but the doorbell rang.

9

Mrs Vanhanen's mother had a full mouth and a fuller figure, and bottle-blonde hair styled in a victory roll. She narrowed her eyes at Hella when she learned what trade she was in, but there was a spark of excitement there too. Hella could tell that the woman loved gossip and was savouring the occasion. "So, what did you want to know?" she asked, as soon as the second round of coffee was served.

"We've been talking about Mr Heikkinen," Hella said cautiously. "Your daughter has been saying some very positive things about him." She glanced at Mrs Vanhanen, who sat there biting her lip and tugging on the gold chain around her neck. "I was wondering if you could tell me a bit more. Do you get on well with him?"

"He's like a son to me! Better, even. Maria was pretty but she was also a daydreamer, an awkward little thing that kept bumping into furniture and lacked practical sense. She always expected everyone to fuss over her. I loved her dearly, of course, she was my child. I was hoping she'd marry well – all mothers do – but I never expected her to marry *that* well! It felt practically like winning a lottery." The woman beamed. "So I told her not to hesitate for a moment, that she could never hope to find a better man.

And luckily she took my advice. Theirs was a happy union indeed, a marriage made in heaven."

Except for the dead baby, Hella thought. Except for the house fire.

"So no skeletons in Mr Heikkinen's closet," she said, smiling. "As expected." She drank the last of her coffee, wondering where to go next. Probably nowhere. If everyone was telling the truth – and why wouldn't they be? – that Johannes Heikkinen seemed like quite a catch.

"Well, there was the cousin…" Mrs Vanhanen piped up.

Hella settled back into the cushions. "Oh yes. The cousin. What can you tell me about him?"

"His name is Veikko Aalto. He is… troubled."

"Always has been," her mother added. "A poet, can you imagine? But I suppose every family has its black sheep. Besides, he was the one who introduced Maria and Johannes, so he had some use."

"Anything I should know about the man, Mrs Vanhanen?"

"No. Not really. It's just that you mentioned skeletons… in closets. This is as close as it gets."

"I don't think this is relevant to a background check on Johannes," the mother said firmly.

Mrs Vanhanen turned several shades of red. "No. I suppose not. Sorry. Just thought I'd mention it, but it's not relevant, of course."

Which, Hella decided as she took her leave, sounded plausible enough. Except for the fact that Mrs Vanhanen was now avoiding her gaze. Each time Hella tried to speak to her, she would look away.

Now, as she walked, Hella thought that she shouldn't have accepted that second helping of cake. Her fitted bodice was straining against her chest, while the belt bit into her stomach. She loosened it up a bit, but even then the dress felt uncomfortable. As if it had shrunk during her hospital stay. And the shoes... Polished to a high gloss and very, very proper, except that her feet must have grown too, because how else could she explain her crunched-up toes and blooming blisters?

Luckily for her, the Surgical Hospital was only a short walk – or hobble – away. And the good thing was that she knew Tom well enough to slide off her shoes in his presence, and even put her feet up on his desk. She smiled at the thought. But when she finally made her way down the foul-smelling corridor, past the mortuary and into Tom's small, cluttered office, she found that same desk covered with a spectacularly precarious arrangement of papers, scientific magazines and misshapen things floating in formaldehyde. Tom was sitting behind the desk, typing with two fingers on a portable Bing. With his heavyweight wrestler's build, he resembled an elegantly dressed circus elephant trying to hit a nail on the head with a tiny hammer.

"Hey, you look *good*," he exclaimed, after a brief glance at her.

"But I feel terrible." Hella cleared the visitors' chair, moving the latest edition of the *Journal of Clinical Pathology*, and slumped into the seat before kicking off her shoes. "My feet are killing me."

"Hmm." Tom frowned, pressing the carriage return lever. "New shoes?"

"Old shoes. New me, I suppose." She screwed up her face, inhaling the smell of death that went back a hundred years. "Couldn't you open a window?"

"Let me see your feet first." Having extracted himself from behind his desk, Tom stooped down to pick up her shoes. "Well, that's easily fixable. Should take less than an hour."

"What are you going to do?"

Tom grinned. "Fill a plastic bag with water, fit it inside the shoe, stick the shoe inside the freezer unit at the mortuary. I got one last month. It's a great invention."

"And then what?"

"Water expands when it turns to ice." Tom shrugged and turned for the door. "Don't look at me like that. You've lived in Lapland, you should know."

Ten minutes later, when Tom came back into the office carrying a tray with two coffee cups, Hella almost succeeded in persuading herself that the idea of her shoes resting next to (or even on top of) some frozen human body was no big deal. Besides, now Tom was obliged to put up with her until the water froze and the sides of her leather pumps stretched. The least he could do to pass the time was answer her questions. She watched as he moved some papers around to create a more or less flat surface on his desk then carefully balanced the coffee tray on top of it.

At last, Tom settled back into his chair with a sigh. "So tell me, dearest, is this a social call?"

"Not really. I'd appreciate your professional advice."

Tom raised an eyebrow. "Did someone die?"

"No." The coffee smelled good and Hella took a sip, not because she wanted more caffeine, but to get rid of the mortuary smell. "Is mental illness hereditary? Genetic?"

"I'm not a psychiatrist." Tom ran a hand through his hair. "Or, if we're being technical, even a real, practising doctor. The people on whom I exercise my skills no longer have any psychological issues. Luckily for me." He grinned at her. "But tell me anyway. What sort of mental illness exactly?"

"The man's father committed suicide, so I presume depression. His cousin is apparently unstable, but I haven't seen him yet."

Tom rested his chin in the palm of his hand. "From what I've heard, depression isn't hereditary. In this country, it's mostly seasonal."

"How so?"

"When November comes and the weather turns dreadful, folks get depressed. Also, you'd be surprised – I was when I first heard this – but people can also become depressed when the sun starts to come up for longer periods of time. It's an adjustment factor."

"Adjustment to sunlight?"

"Apparently." Tom shrugged. "It's like they hold firm while the nights are long and there's no sun, then all of a sudden there's a backlash."

Maybe that was her problem too, Hella thought. Too much sun and she became depressed. Maybe that was the reason she wasn't sleeping. Maybe it had nothing to do with her "accident" or the fact that she had moved into her murdered parents' house.

"What else?" she asked. "It can't just be sunlight."

"There's this book," Tom said. "It's called the *DSM*, the *Diagnostic and Statistical Manual of Mental Disorders*. It was published last year, but we've only just got it. One of my colleagues has it. If you want me to, I can borrow it and check." He put his empty coffee cup back on the tray. "So, what's this all about, a new investigation?"

"Kind of." Hella sighed. "I feel like I'm wasting my time. So far, nothing I've learned seems even remotely interesting. But Jokela was insistent, and he's paying good money, so I can't help wondering —"

"Jokela?" Tom said. "Don't tell me *he* hired you?"

"It's nothing, Tom. He's probably just trying to support me. Easy money, you know." Hella smiled at her friend. "There seems to be nothing criminal here, nothing whatsoever. The man I'm doing a background check on lost his child and his wife, and I thought there might be something in it, but the baby died in hospital, from a weak heart."

Tom leaned forward. "What about the wife?"

"There was a fire. Apparently the husband was badly burned trying to save her."

"Hmm," Tom said. "You want me to check his case history? I can do that easily enough if you give me the name."

"Heikkinen. Johannes Heikkinen."

Tom glanced at her sharply. He opened his mouth to speak, then thought better of it.

"What is it?"

"Nothing. Heikkinen, you said?" He scribbled the name on one of the envelopes littering his desk. "Come back the day after tomorrow and I'll tell you what I've got on him." He looked at his wristwatch and rose. "I'll go and get your shoes now. But Hella —"

"What?"

"Please be careful. You think it all sounds harmless, but you know Jokela – he wouldn't recognize danger if it was served to him on a plate with some curly parsley stuck in its mouth. He might sincerely believe that what he entrusted you with is your average, run-of-the-mill background check. But Hella, you and I, we know better."

"Don't be so melodramatic." She laughed. "I *promise* it'll all be fine."

But Tom's face remained serious. "Promise me you'll be careful, all right?"

10

There are two very different types of detective, Hella thought as she emerged from the gloomy underbelly of the Surgical Hospital. Her ice-cold shoes felt like ointment on her feet, and she started walking downhill at a brisk trot. There are the hunters and the gatherers, much like our Stone Age ancestors, the former men of action and the latter of reflection. Philip Marlowe was a hunter. Sherlock Holmes and Hercule Poirot were gatherers, poring over the little clues. And what was she? Now that she had collected a few meagre morsels of information, was she supposed to withdraw to her room with a glass of sherry and a violin and simply let her little grey cells go to work until she emerged with a solution? But a solution to what? She didn't even know if there *was* anything worth looking at. Tom had told her depression wasn't hereditary. Everyone she had met, including the sister and mother of the man's wife, had nothing but praise for Heikkinen. The fact that he had a crazy cousin didn't mean anything. Hella knew that the best course of action would be to go home, clear the dust that had settled on her father's ancient typewriter and write up a report, concluding that there were no worrisome elements or signs in the deportment or personality of Mr Johannes Heikkinen. She glanced at her wristwatch. It was 4 p.m. She would do just that. Before that, though, she'd take a detour by Puu-Vallila and try to strike up a conversation with Mr Veikko Aalto. No harm in meeting the cousin and making sure.

The Puu-Vallila neighbourhood was up-and-coming. Driven by the lack of affordable housing, more and more office workers from central Helsinki were buying timber houses in what had originally been a working-class area. With their high gambrel roofs, bay windows and wooden facades, the houses looked rather like small villas, and now every other house sported a fresh coat of paint in some cheery colour: ochre, red, emerald green. On Virtaintie, only a few of the homes looked worse for wear. And only one, number five, squeezed between a pale green number and its salmon-pink twin, looked like a decaying tooth in an otherwise bright smile. Hella walked past it without stopping. Out of a corner of her eye, she glimpsed the twitch of a grey net curtain, a pale shadow behind it. She had initially intended to ring the doorbell and simply introduce herself to Mr Aalto, but the house, with its grimy windows and its paint flaking off like dandruff… On impulse, she climbed the porch of the house next door instead, number seven, and pressed the doorbell. Here lived the man who had contacted the police about Aalto. Mäkinen? Koskinen? She searched her memory for his name, before remembering she had jotted it down in her notebook. Sopanen. That was it. Given the police report, Hella supposed Mr Sopanen might be inclined to talk.

The man who answered the doorbell was fiftyish, short and pink, with a little twitching moustache and small button-bright eyes framed by rimless spectacles. He was wearing a neat linen suit and a shirt with a tie. His formal appearance jarred with the loud striped wallpaper and children's toys scattered around the front room, but Hella reasoned that he must have just got home from work. There was a well-worn leather briefcase on a chair by the door.

The man looked at her inquiringly. "Are you a friend of my daughter's? I'm sorry, but I can't quite place you."

Hella showed him her PI card. "This is about your neighbour, Mr Aalto."

Immediately, he nodded as if he'd been expecting her. "Of course. Do come in."

Sidestepping a child's tricycle, a dolls' pram and a tiny plastic cart – Mr Sopanen seemed to be living in a toy store – she followed him into a nice, clean kitchen that smelled of milk and cardamom. "Coffee?" the man asked. Without waiting for her answer, he picked up a child-sized mug, filled it and placed it in front of her on the table. "What did he do now, kill another dog?"

"Dog?"

"I suppose that means the answer is no," Mr Sopanen said, sitting down with a sigh. "So Tessu was the only one. The only one we know of, that is."

Hella looked at her coffee. This would be her seventh cup of the day, and she didn't feel like drinking it. But that would be impolite, so she took a sip anyway. "What happened to Tessu?"

The man shrugged. "There was a hole in the fence, and that stupid pup kept going over to Aalto's house." He turned his head to look at the prim little garden at the back of his own house, then cleared his throat. "But I thought Aalto loved dogs. He'd play with it, save it a bone. Always so nice and so friendly. And then, one day…"

Mr Sopanen was still looking away, a pained expression on his small face. Hella waited.

"And then, one day, I saw that bastard feeding Tessu something that looked like a steak. And I should have thought more about it, should have asked him why he was giving steak to a Labrador when he himself was as poor as a church mouse, but… but I didn't. Not that it would have changed anything, it was already too late for that, but still." The man was looking at Hella now, his gaze pleading for understanding. "Only how could I have known? I thought he loved Tessu. He could have told me if my dog was bothering him, I'd have repaired the hole in the fence."

"There was no way you could have known," Hella said. "So Tessu died after eating the steak. Did you confront Mr Aalto about it?"

"I did." The man shrugged. "He denied everything. He was practically foaming at the mouth, told me he had nothing to do with my stupid dog. But I know what I saw." He half-turned towards the window again, pulled back a curtain. "I buried Tessu in the garden, put a big stone on his grave and a statue of a dog that I commissioned from a sculptor. Cost me a tenth of my monthly wage, but I wanted the bastard to have to see it from his porch every time he went outside."

Hella nodded. From where she was sitting, she could see a bronze sculpture of a dog, life-sized, head raised. "When did it happen?"

"Just about five years ago." The small pink man picked up his coffee cup again. "He was always nice enough before that, just an ordinary neighbour, but he's got much worse since. Sometimes he screams all night, other days he yells at me from over the fence. I've thought about moving, but who'd buy next to him?" Mr Sopanen, his tight little mouth pursed and eyes narrowed, stared at the desolate garden.

"Anyway. If you're not here about a murdered dog, then what are you looking for?"

Hella thought about what the officer in the police archives had said about Veikko Aalto. *No criminal record. Petty mischief.* But killing dogs wasn't petty mischief, it was *evil*, and she thought she knew the answer to Mr Sopanen's question. She could answer it in one word: *trouble*.

11

If detective work was gathering, then Veikko Aalto was a natural at it. Only instead of clues and evidence, he gathered whatever junk he could find. Broken picture frames. Light bulbs. Umbrellas. Bedsprings. He piled them up on every available surface, blocking the view out of the front window. The room smelled of mould and ammonia. It was crawling with things Hella preferred not to name. Maybe *gathering* wasn't the right word. Maybe the word was *hoarding*.

As her eyes struggled to adjust to the gloom after the bright sunshine outside, more junk came to the fore, all of it covered with grey fur. In this house, even the furniture played along, gathering dust.

"What did you say your name was?" His voice sounded scratchy, as if he hadn't used it in a long time.

She gave him her name again, slowly and carefully, her eyes searching his face for some telltale sign of madness, whatever that might be. Dark hair. Blue eyes. Straight nose, strong chin. Veikko Aalto must have been handsome once, a long time ago. Now, he looked as thin and prickly as barbed wire, his face all sharp angles.

"What's this about?"

"I'm here because of your cousin, Johannes. You know where he works, right?"

A doubtful, puzzled look came over his face. "But you went next door first."

"True," Hella said. "I made a mistake. A silly one. That small pink gentleman – I thought he was you."

"He must have told you about his dog." He said it like a statement of fact.

Hella glanced out of the back window, at the back yard next door that she could see over the picket fence, and the bronze Labrador facing her, jaws gaping open. No matter how much junk he collected, you could still see the statue from Veikko Aalto's living room.

"I liked that dog," the man said. His gaze was needling her now, as if he was pretending, as if he was smart and cunning rather than simply evil. "Why are you asking about my cousin?"

"Well," Hella smiled bravely. "It's a pure formality. I'm doing a background check on him. You know how these things go." She hoped that he would leave it at that, but no such luck.

"So, who *are* you?" His voice sounded hoarse. "What do you want with my cousin?"

Hella repeated her lie. "I'm a secretary in the SUPO's personnel department." In a way, the latter part of the sentence was true, because detective work *was* all about meeting people. Nice people, like Mrs Vanhanen with her poodle hair and her stewed prunes, crazy people like Veikko Aalto. She didn't need Tom's reference manual to know that this man was truly and certifiably mad.

"Oh. I thought you might want to marry him."

"No."

There was a silence. "I'm a poet," Veikko Aalto finally

said. "You didn't ask, but I'm telling you just in case." He rubbed his hands together. "So, what do you want to know?"

"I was hoping you could tell me about your cousin," Hella said. "What sort of a man he is. I understand you're his only living family?"

"I am." The man sat down, right onto a heap of rags that covered an old sofa. "If he dies, I'll inherit his apartment." For some reason, the thought made him laugh. Hella waited. There was a collection of picture frames on a console behind him, all but two of them empty. Of the two photographs, one was of Mata Hari. The other was of a smiling girl in a traditional costume. A cockroach was running along its frame. Veikko Aalto stopped laughing. "My cousin is a bad man. I do not see Johannes often." He swiped his tongue over his cracked lips. "I'm afraid I can't tell you anything."

"That's all right," Hella said brightly. She had seen more than enough. The air in the room, damp and sickening, was making her dizzy. "I'd better go now." Before I faint, she thought. Why had she even come here? There was nothing to be said about Johannes Heikkinen, nothing at all.

She rushed out of the house, her heart hammering away in her throat. It was like emerging from a cave: the clean street air had never seemed so sweet, the sunshine so mellow. On the corner of Sturenkatu, there was a Karl Fazer shop. Hella went inside with the intention of buying some chocolate, but changed her mind as soon as she saw what was on offer on the counter. "I'll have a big packet of *salmiakki*," she said. The sharp, pungent smell of the liquorice candy was exactly what she needed. Plump and apple-cheeked, the sales girl smiled at Hella. "Excellent choice. We only started making these recently, but they've been a huge success. You'll come again, I'm sure."

Maybe, Hella thought. Though not here. She shivered, thinking of that awful house, and the poor dead Labrador Tessu. Tomorrow, she'd take her report to Jokela, and then she'd try her best to forget all about it.

12

There was an envelope waiting for her on the doormat. On top of it rested a piece of paper torn out of a yellow lined notebook, folded in two and secured with a pebble so that it wouldn't fly away in the wind. Hella picked that up first.

Dearest neighbour, the note read, the handwriting small and neat.

> Just wanted to tell you that there was some tramp who kept peering into your windows this afternoon. I saw him as I was coming home from work. And I know that as a former police officer you are perfectly capable of taking care of yourself, but still I chased him away, and told him I'd break his neck if I ever saw him again. I also wanted to tell you that I had a great time last night. If the feeling's mutual, how about another dinner later this week?
>
> E.K.

Hella pocketed the note. The envelope she took inside and set it down on the coffee table, next to the parcel she had received the other day. Then, with a contented sigh, she kicked off her shoes.

With the curtains drawn, and the honey-coloured evening light softening the edges of the furniture, the living room looked almost cosy and inviting. Hella closed her eyes, imagining how it might feel to go back in time, to the day before her parents, sister and nephew left for the last time to visit the summer cabin. Smell is a memory, too, and she could feel it all now: wood polish, soap and cinnamon. Her mother sprinkled cinnamon on literally everything. And then there were the sounds: birdsong, pots banging against one another, water running from the tap, floorboards squeaking, all the small noises of everyday life that you never heard when you lived alone. Her mother would have been in the kitchen, baking something, probably the sort of Åland pancake Hella had eaten this very morning. Her father, who could never sit still, would be pacing the room, dropping ashes from his cigarette into the barbed-wire-framed plate he used as an ashtray. And Christina... Christina would be upstairs, singing Matti to sleep. *Nuku nuku nurmilintu, sleep, sleep, grassland bird.* Executed in a high falsetto voice – Christina was never much of a singer, just like the rest of the family – but Matti loved that song, and that was all that mattered.

Hella opened her eyes, and her gaze fell on the letter. No one knew she lived here, except for Jokela and Steve. And Erkki. She slid open the flap on the envelope. The letter was short, a couple of lines. Good, expensive paper, blue ink.

Dear Miss Mauzer,

I understand you don't have a telephone, so I have no choice but to write to you. If it is not too much trouble, would you be so kind as to come and see me at home,

any day this week before nine in the morning. I promise
I won't take up too much of your time.

    Sincerely,

        Johannes Heikkinen

P.S. I believe you already know my address.

She set the letter back down. So, the news had already
got around. She wondered who had told him. The greengrocer, the neighbour who had showed her the room to
let? She had never given them her name, or her address,
but Heikkinen was a spy, and people in his trade prided
themselves on knowing things before everyone else. Or
it could have been someone at Headquarters, that was
certainly possible too. Maybe even Mrs Vanhanen or her
mother; the stamp on the envelope showed that the letter
had been posted at noon that day. Not that it mattered.

Hella stared at the envelope for a long time, trying to
make up her mind about it. If she denied everything, he
simply wouldn't believe her. Heikkinen wouldn't have
written to her if he wasn't sure. A better course of action
would be to go and talk to him. She didn't think he'd be
aggressive – she was more worried about the tramp that
Erkki had spotted peering through her windows. Was he
the one who'd left her the strange package with its stained
tissue and a list of numbers? And if yes, was he dangerous?
There was no way of knowing.

That night, when Hella went to bed, she fell asleep as soon
as her head touched the pillow. Far from being restful, her
sleep was full of nightmares. There was a large yellow dog
that Hella thought might be Tessu, and a vagabond with
his dirty hands cupped to the window, trying to sneak a
peek into her living room. There was a cockroach running

along a picture frame, and the beefy officer from Archives, his cornflower-blue eyes staring at her in disapproval as he tore her parents' file to pieces. There was Jokela, looking smug, and Veikko Aalto, looking lost, and a monstrous Sisu truck skidding out of control on a narrow country road. And then, just before she woke up screaming, she saw her mother's body flying through the warm April night, and Matti's navy lace-up booties, and the wheel of his stroller that, for a moment, was as big as the moon.

13

Having woken from her nightmare at two in the morning, Hella couldn't get back to sleep. The night was full of noises, and she spent the rest of it leaping up and checking everything: the bolts, the door, the windows, and the milky dusk beyond, full of deep shadows and trembling lights. It was a good thing she hadn't yet had a telephone line installed, because otherwise she might have turned into a damsel in distress; she might have called Steve, and begged him to come and sleep in the spare room. The thought made her squirm – she always thought of herself as being tough as nails – but maybe it was simply not true, maybe in reality she was weak but too proud to admit it.

Finally, recognizing the futility of staying in bed, she grabbed the moth-eaten nightgown that used to belong to her sister and shuffled downstairs. Her body was one hard knot of pain, her jaw clamped so tight that her teeth ached. Moving slowly, like an old lady with arthritis, she heated water and prepared a big pot of coffee. Then, setting it next to her father's ancient typewriter, she began to type her report. Once that was done, she'd also ask Jokela to investigate the disappearance of her parents' file from the archives.

At quarter past seven, washed and dressed in her one skirt suit, she stood waiting at the tram stop for the number 5 light yellow line from Etu-Töölö to Katajanokka. When it arrived, it was already chock-full with office employees rushing to get to work. She managed to find a seat in the last row, where she was squeezed between a girl who spent her time straightening her nylon stockings and a man puffing on a foul-smelling cigar. Hella fished the tin of *salmiakki* out of her handbag and popped one into her mouth. The tram rocked, the city unfolding before her eyes. It looked unused to so much sunshine, its soft, washed-out colours more natural when drenched in fog. As the tram approached the market square, she opened the window so that she could smell the sea, the salty tang of it, like liquorice, and feel the sunshine caressing her face.

Hella climbed out at Katajanokka, the tram empty now except for the cigar-smoking man. She glanced at her wristwatch: it was 7.40. They'd have plenty of time to talk before Heikkinen had to leave for work at nine. She decided she wouldn't bother asking him how he knew she was investigating him – he wouldn't tell anyway, and it didn't really matter.

She was crossing the Katajanokka canal when she heard the voice calling her. "My dear child! Fancy seeing you here! And all dressed up." Hella stopped in her tracks, swallowing a curse.

"Mr Kyander." Running into him was not a surprise, or at least it shouldn't have been. Kyander, her father's closest friend and colleague, lived in Katajanokka, and she had walked past his house only two days ago. Still, she had hoped not to run into him, to never see him again after he'd refused to help her last year. She turned and looked at him. The man was beaming, his mouth stretched wide, his bald scalp as shiny as the rest of his fat old face. He took her hand in both of his. "So, what brings you here?"

"Work," Hella said curtly, hoping he'd get the hint.

"Young people." Kyander let out a peal of laughter. "With you, it's always work, work, work, it's all you ever talk about." He pulled a handkerchief the size of a small sail out of his pocket and wiped his forehead with it. "I'm done with working. I'll be taking my retirement next month, and tomorrow I'm heading out to look at a couple of cabins by Lake Saimaa. You should come and visit me there one day."

Not a chance in hell, Hella thought.

"You do look well, though," Kyander said pensively. "I wanted to visit you in hospital when I heard about your accident, I really did. I even bought a box of chocolates. But when I called them, a couple of weeks later, you were gone."

"I went to stay with friends in Lapland." She glanced at her wristwatch. "I'm sorry, but I need to go now. I have an appointment."

"Then you must promise to come and see me one day. Will you? We'll talk about your father. I've started writing my memoirs, you know. A lot of things I can't share, of course, but what I *can* share is still pretty exciting stuff."

"All right," Hella said. Anything to get rid of him. She turned away and quickened her step. Don't count on it, she thought. I never want to see you again, ever.

At eight sharp, she was standing on Heikkinen's doorstep, pressing her finger on the bell. She did not know what to expect. A pleasant, quiet widower who was also a gifted pianist? A good neighbour and a perfect son-in-law? A spy, about to be promoted to be the new head of the homicide squad? All of these at once, most likely.

It was his hands that she noticed first. Beautiful hands, with long, sensitive fingers. A wedding band. A gold watch on a narrow wrist. A dazzling white shirt. Then the intelligent, fine-boned face, the hooded lids, the white hair in rapid retreat over a high forehead.

"Miss Mauzer." He extended a hand for her to shake. "It is a pleasure to meet you. Do come in."

She followed him inside. It was a beautiful, expensively appointed home, the parquet floors covered in faded oriental rugs, the tall narrow windows framed by heavy silk curtains. The living room was painted a daffodil yellow, and was sparsely furnished. A tray was set out on a side table, with coffee, pancakes, honey and a bowl of fruit, a fat orange cat sitting next to it like a sentinel. Heikkinen poured coffee and handed her a cup. It was made of the finest porcelain, as thin and translucent as a sheet of paper.

"So, what are you going to tell them?" Heikkinen was smiling. "Did I pass the test?"

As she had expected, he didn't ask who had hired her. The whole conversation felt surreal, two friends meeting over coffee for some chit-chat. Was it a role he was playing? The cat made a figure eight around her shins, nudging her with its head.

Hella smiled. "I don't know about a test. Is there anything you wanted to talk to me about?"

"As a matter of fact, there is." He looked at her pensively. "You know, when I found out that you were asking questions about me, I was upset about it at first. Not because I don't see the value in background checks – I've done a number of them myself – but because I knew that you'd hear about my son, and my wife, and that you'd immediately jump to conclusions. And you did. I know you did. This was why I asked you to come by. So that I can tell you about Maria myself. Here she is."

Without taking his eyes off Hella, he reached for a photograph on the bookshelf behind him. It showed a small, grey woman with a worried face and a knitted shawl over her shoulders. Not a match for her handsome, presentable husband, but ill-assorted couples were more common than everyone thought. It didn't necessarily mean anything.

Hella thought about what Mrs Vanhanen had said, about how Maria's widower still left her slippers by her side of the bed, how he kept her lily of the valley perfume in the bathroom. She handed back the photograph. "I did wonder about that, yes. What happened exactly? I understand it was some sort of accident?"

"It was my fault," he sighed. "No matter what anyone says. Five years have passed, but I can't stop thinking about it. I should have been there for her." His gaze clouded. "Maria was a voracious reader. She was also a very anxious person, the sort who didn't like to go outside. It's why we always painted the rooms yellow, so that she could have some light, or at least the illusion of it. Anyway. One day, the power went off in the neighbourhood. She wanted to read in bed, as was her habit, so she lit a candle, and then she fell asleep. I know because my cousin Veikko was visiting that evening, and she had told him that was what she was planning to do. He was the last person to see her alive." Heikkinen swallowed, closed his eyes. His voice, when he spoke again, sounded hoarse. "I was working late that night, some stupid committee on cross-border cooperation that dragged on for hours, and when I got home, I saw the smoke, and a line of neighbours passing buckets of water. No one had thought to go inside. So I pressed my scarf to my nose and I went in. I thought that Maria might be hiding somewhere, terrified and disoriented, that I could still bring her out. I thought I could save her, I really did."

Heikkinen's voice caught. He took a deep breath. "But it was too late. *I* was too late."

"I'm sorry," Hella said.

He looked at her. "You cannot imagine how that feels. When you spend your entire career helping people but cannot protect the ones closest to you? My child first, and then my wife? What am I good for if I couldn't save *them?*"

He turned, facing the windows. There were metal bars on them, Hella noticed, but it *was* a ground-floor apartment.

Heikkinen was still talking. "You can write that in your report, all of it. I have nothing to be ashamed of, career-wise, but this —" She saw his shoulders rise. "Excuse me." He pulled a handkerchief out of his trouser pocket, pressed it to his face. "The cat survived," he said, through the handkerchief. "It escaped when the neighbours broke the door down, and it stayed away for a while, but it came back, eventually. She loved that cat." His body shook.

Hella stood up. The grandfather clock in the corner was pointing to a quarter to nine. She cleared her throat, feeling awkward. "Thank you for your time, sir. For your trust, too. I should be going now."

"Wait," Heikkinen said. He sighed. "There's something else." He turned to face her. "Something that I wanted to ask *you*. Are you, by any chance, Colonel Mauzer's daughter?"

14

"What did you say?" Tom asked.

"The truth." Sitting by the small window in Tom's office, Hella could glimpse the grass speckled with tiny daisies and, beyond, the feet of visitors shuffling towards the hospital's entrance. Heat was shimmering above the pavement. "Heikkinen knew my father, apparently. They worked together on some covert operation back in the day, though of course he didn't tell me which one." She shrugged. "Well, given how small the Finnish secret service is, it wasn't that much of a surprise."

Tom raised his eyebrows. "Maybe not a surprise, but you still seem troubled."

"Do I? Maybe because he asked if I knew who killed my family. He didn't say it like that, but that's what he meant."

"Such a tactless thing to ask." Tom shook his head. "You poor thing. I'm not sure that you moving back into the family home was such a great idea. Anyway." He pointed to a large volume on his desk. "I borrowed the *DSM*, and apparently depression and schizophrenia *can* run in families."

"I don't think he has either," Hella said. "Do you have anything else for me?"

Tom rested his hand on a slim cardboard file. "This is everything I could find on Mr and Mrs Heikkinen. Rather interesting reading, actually. And, as a matter of fact, there *was* a small investigation at the time of the incident. People from the SUPO wanted to make sure it was an accident all right."

"And was it?"

He paused. "Maybe not exactly." He licked his index finger and turned the page. "Poor Mr Heikkinen really did risk his life trying to pull his other half from the inferno. He suffered some serious burns, and he was unconscious for a while. And it seems that the fire started accidentally."

"*Seems?*" Hella said.

"It's possible that Maria Heikkinen was an especially heavy sleeper," Tom said, "but usually people wake up when a fire breaks out in the room where they're sleeping. Unless..." He frowned and bent over the file.

"Unless they're already unconscious by the time the fire starts."

"Exactly."

She felt a familiar tingling in her hands, her heart skipping a beat, the adrenaline rushing through her body. Maybe all detectives got the same feeling when they were on a case and suddenly, suddenly, there was *something*. "Murder?"

"Suicide, more likely." Tom picked up a document from the file, slid it towards her. He was looking away, not meeting her eye. "From what it says here, the lady had been depressed for a while and lived on sleeping pills and tranquillizers. Promethazine, phenobarbital... that sort of thing. It also says her baby died two years before, to the day, so no wonder."

The document Tom gave her was a toxicology report. It listed the chemical elements present in Maria Heikkinen's blood at the time of her death, and, in bold, their concentration, all of them many times above the normal level.

"The report is signed by you," Hella said, surprised.

"That's because I was the one who performed an autopsy on her." Tom closed the file. "I forgot all about it. It only started coming back to me when I saw the file."

Hella stared. "You can't forget a thing like that. This city's not New York. Not Paris or Bombay either. How many autopsies do you perform in a year? Look at me, Tom."

He threw his hands up in the air. "All right, I didn't tell you the truth just now. I remembered that case as soon as you mentioned it the other day. Not the sort of thing you can forget easily. But I wasn't proud of myself. I hadn't been my usual diligent self on that one, due to personal circumstances. Well, you know all about my personal circumstances."

"I do." Hella nodded. "So you think it could have been murder? When I spoke to her mother, she said Maria was a helpless little thing who was always bumping into furniture. I wondered if her husband was beating her, and her clumsiness was an excuse."

"No." Tom leafed through the file, frowning. "There was some bruising, both recent – could have happened while she was being rescued – and old, too, but if the mother says her daughter was clumsy, that could be just it." Tom closed the file with a snap. "Besides, if the husband was the killer, then why would he have pulled her body out of the fire? It would have been so much easier for him to let her burn. There would have been no proof, no evidence." Tom hauled himself out of his chair with a groan, and opened the window. "The heat in here, I'm not used to it. They say it'll last, too."

"So you think I'm wrong to suspect him," Hella said.

"It certainly looks that way. Both the woman's mother and her sister testified that poor Maria had anxiety attacks, and what they called 'sad and irrational spells'. They mentioned that she couldn't sleep, either, and was taking pills."

"And the drugs found in her blood" – Hella glanced at the list – "promethazine and phenobarbital were what her doctor had prescribed her?"

"Promethazine, yes. The drug's actually an antihistamine, most commonly used for allergies, but it binds to receptors in the brain and causes sleepiness and sedation. It's what they give patients before surgery. Maria Heikkinen had a fancy doctor, and he prescribed it to her all right. Not the phenobarbital, though. That one, well, no one knows how she came by it, and that was what bothered me at the time. But in the end, I told myself that given the thriving black market since the war ended, it can't have been difficult for Maria to find it. Luminal, as it's called, is a common drug and has been around for decades. The Nazis euthanized disabled children with it."

Hella shivered. "So you knew about the phenobarbital but still left it at that," she said.

Tom rolled his eyes. "I didn't *leave* it anywhere. It wasn't my job. The SUPO said they thought it might have been suicide – or an accidental overdose, that's also possible – but because Mr Heikkinen wanted to give his wife a decent funeral, they didn't push it further."

"I see."

Tom smiled. "That's the homicide detective in you talking. But I didn't find any evidence of murder. All the witness statements said in essence the same thing: she was a woman who was still suffering after the loss of her only child, and who needed drugs to keep on living. Whether she took too much accidentally or on purpose is open to interpretation, but it ends there. It's not because there are some loose ends that my conclusion is any different."

Hella thought back to her interview with Maria's sister. *That poor baby, they didn't even have time to name him. Maria died two years after that, to the day.*

"You're probably right," she said.

"*But?*" Tom grinned. "Knowing you, this is just the beginning."

"There's no *but*." She picked up the file from his desk. "I'll add another page to my report for Jokela, and that's it. I have better things to do." Like looking for my family's killer, she thought.

15

She had barely had enough time to dump her groceries on the kitchen table – rye bread, butter, a chunk of beef to make meatballs, lingonberry jam and potatoes –when someone knocked on her door. Maybe it was Erkki, she thought hopefully, remembering the note he had left her the previous day. If he asked her out to dinner again, then she wouldn't have to cook. But when she opened the door, it was Steve she saw. He was smiling.

"Hello, Sherlock! How's your investigation progressing?"

"It's over," Hella said. "I only need to finish typing up the report, and then I'm done."

"Good." Steve's smile became even brighter. "Then how about we go out to dinner? I have some news. I thought we could perhaps go to that little red café on the waterfront, you know the one I'm talking about? It's not far from here, and at this time of the year it's really nice."

Hella almost said *I know*, then thought better of it. The prospect of returning to the cafe was alluring, but going there with Steve was out of the question. Instead she said: "I've just bought food, you can come in and help me cook."

Steve grinned. "With pleasure, though I'm not sure

that's an accurate way of describing it. How about we do the usual: *I* cook and you sit and watch?"

She followed him into the kitchen, where Steve tied one of her mother's aprons around his waist before taking a cast-iron pan off a hook, wiping it with a dish towel and placing it on the stove. He greased the pan with butter then looked around. "Seen a meat grinder anywhere?"

"I think there's one in the cupboard." She stifled a yawn. "So what's your big news?"

"Later, child. Got any onions?"

Hella, who never knew meatball recipes included onions, shook her head.

"Any spice?"

"There's some on the rack, I believe."

Now it was Steve's turn to shake his head. "It's turned into a rock. I'd need a pickaxe to break this down."

"Then we'll have to do without." She fought to stifle another yawn. "It's the meat that counts, right?"

Hands on his hips, Steve turned and stared. "I hope that's not the way you conduct your investigations, Private Eye Mauzer! 'Oh, I couldn't find the murder weapon, but we'll just have to do without it, it's the dead body that counts.' I mean, seriously?"

"It's just salt," Hella said lamely.

"Yep, it's just salt, and onion and pepper and allspice. And without all that, the meat *and* the potatoes are going to taste disgusting. Got a hammer, by any chance?"

"I've got a gun. You can use that to crush salt, I suppose. Or, I don't know, you can run it through the meat grinder?" There was something hovering at the edge of her consciousness, something that Steve had said about murder weapons, but Hella couldn't quite put her finger on it. "What? Did you say something?"

"I said, now that's an idea." Steve ran a piece of rye bread through the grinder to clean it of any lingering meat residue, then put a lump of salt into it. "What are you chewing?"

"*Salmiakki.* Got them from the Karl Fazer store yesterday." Hella showed him the tin, which was already half-empty. "Want some?"

"No thanks." But Steve still picked up the tin, turned it over in his hands. "Do you know where the name *salmiakki* comes from?"

"No idea."

"*Sal ammoniac,* ammonia salts in Latin. You can wake the dead with it. That stuff is used as fertilizer or animal food."

"Whatever," Hella said. "I like it. It tastes rather good."

"Most of it comes from Egypt and is the product of burned camel droppings."

"Really?"

"That's what they say."

Hella picked up another lozenge, studied it carefully, then stuffed it into her mouth. "I don't care."

"I can see that. All right, now that the meatballs are sorted, do you know how to peel potatoes?"

"Are you making fun of me?" Hella picked up the knife. "You know me better than that."

For a moment, neither of them spoke. The meatballs sizzled in the pan, and the big pot of salted water that Steve had put on the hob was starting to boil. Hella dropped the potatoes into it, one at a time.

"Seriously, though," Steve said, his back to her. "How did we end up like this? I thought you and I... That we would —"

"That we would what?" It came out harsher than she had intended.

"I don't know. Live together. Get married. Have a child."

"You already have a child," Hella said dully. "I don't know how many times you reminded me of that. And, until recently, you also had a wife you had no intention of leaving."

"But I finally did. At about the same time you told me that you and I didn't have a future together." Steve turned to face her. "I still don't understand how that happened. How it was just *over*, so suddenly."

"Some days, I think *over* is not the right word." Hella put a lid on the pan. "For something to be *over*, that something first needs to get *started*. What we had between us was mostly me waiting for you to make up your mind. Months that turned into years, and I was still there, and still waiting. Always on my best behaviour, because you don't catch flies with vinegar, right? All that time waiting, and planning, and hoping. And... nothing." Hella snorted. "I'd be the world champion of waiting if it was an Olympic sport. And besides, I discovered that I quite liked your wife. That she didn't deserve any of it."

"I'm not going back to Elsbeth," Steve said.

"That's stupid, but that's your problem. Not mine."

"Hella, I..." Steve ran a hand through his hair. "I understand that you're mad at me. You have every right to be. But I'd like you to think about this."

"I have."

"Maybe we could —"

"Stop. You'll ruin dinner. And by the way, the meatballs look about ready."

Steve glanced at the stove, as if he'd forgotten what it was they were doing. There was a silence, and then he said, "I'm not hungry any more. Enjoy your food."

The front door banged shut, sending shivers through the old wooden house. Slowly, Hella picked up a fork, stabbed one of the meatballs and put it in her mouth. It tasted good. Maybe it would have been even better if they'd added onion, but onions made you cry and she didn't want that. She wiped her eyes on her sleeve. All this was ridiculous. She shouldn't have let him into the house. And Steve hadn't even told her his big news. She was briefly tempted to run after him, but then she wondered what good that would do. They weren't getting back together. And maybe it wasn't his fault, maybe the fault was with her; why otherwise would she have dumped him right when he finally became available?

Because she'd never really believed that *happily ever after* was the thing. You couldn't believe in that when all it took was one Sisu truck and one driver to wipe out a happy family. She sniffed, heard her father's voice in her ears. Stern, yet with a hint of amusement. *Now, I won't have you crying over a man. Back straight. Chin up.* Hella sniffed and wiped her eyes with the heel of her hand. "This is nothing, Pa," she whispered. "Really, it's nothing. Just a little heartbreak, but I'm used to it. I'll eat now, and then I'll keep on looking for your killer."

16

What better time than a night flooded with midnight sun to confront your worst fears?

What better place than a family home where every nook and corner and squeaky floorboard holds memories of the child you had once been, of the trust and optimism you had once felt?

What better company than yourself?

After doing the dishes, Hella cleared the kitchen table and opened her notebook on a new page.

She had decided she was going to investigate her family's deaths as if they had happened to other people, some other family, people she pitied but didn't know. It was easier that way, it put things into perspective. So: Mr M, Mrs M, young C and child. And, for the first time in her life, she was going to think of it as murder, not an accident like everyone always said. Because what had been bothering her was this: if it had been an accident, why would the file at the police archives be empty?

The facts were simple.

On the morning of 16 April 1942, while their country was fighting the Continuation War against the Soviet Union to recover lost Finnish territories, and while their unwanted allies the Nazis were becoming increasingly present on Helsinki streets, the M family took a train to Parola. Their intention was to look at a summer cabin they were hoping to buy, set on the shores of Lake Lehijärvi. Anyone could have known they were going there, because they'd mentioned it often enough. They had arrived at the cabin in the early hours of the afternoon, liked what they saw and made an offer to buy, which was accepted on the spot. Then the M family started to walk back to the station.

Here Hella paused, thinking. As far as she knew, the M family hadn't specifically mentioned which train they were planning to take to get back to the city, but that was easy enough to find, too – there were only a few trains at that time of year. So anyone who might have wanted to kill the M family could have done it very simply, and they could have made it look like an accident.

The big question was, why would anybody want to kill them?

Mrs M was a housewife. She liked baking and knitting, and playing hide-and-seek with her grandson. She dreamed of travelling to Italy one day and visiting the Uffizi gallery. She always refused to share the recipe for her Russian coulibiac – her signature dish – with anyone, even her daughters. Why would anyone want to kill a woman like her? Hella sighed, massaging her temples. It just made no sense.

The child? She could still picture him sleeping, damp blonde curls plastered to his cheek, one small, plump hand open, the other gripping the ear of a knitted moose. Not him. No one would have wanted to kill him.

The child's mother, C, her sister and best friend. C was unmarried and unemployed, but she was the most optimistic person Hella had ever known. C loved sewing new clothes, the colour yellow, and dancing. She wore berets in the winter because she thought they made her look sophisticated, like a Parisian. Hella set down her pen, her eyes full of tears. It must have been a terrible accident, that's all. The driver lost control of his vehicle. Panicked. Abandoned the truck – it was found in Parola the following day. Police later told Hella that the truck had been stolen from the Finlayson cotton factory in Tampere. It must have been a teenager, a kid, or someone who'd done it on a dare. If that was the case, she would simply have to accept that she would never know. Hella forced herself to pick up her pen.

On to Mr M now. Colonel Niklas M. Chain-smoker, card-player, the best spy of his generation, a man who could also imitate bird whistles and made the most delicious hot chocolate. He'd been killed just before he was due to take early retirement, which was absurd, but Hella knew that, unlike in novels, things didn't stop happening in real life simply because they failed to make sense.

She popped another lozenge into her mouth and thought about Steve. Her relationship with him made no sense either, just like the fact that she still loved him, that she had never loved anyone but him. She'd be better off with someone else, someone she didn't expect so much from. Hella looked out of the window at Erkki Kanerva's house. His curtains were drawn. Had he seen her earlier, cooking with Steve? If yes, would he show up on her doorstep again?

For a long time after her family's deaths, she couldn't talk or even think about what had happened. Every time she tried, words failed her. Her mind went blank and numb. She had heard what the kindly inspector told her, but it hadn't registered. A tragic accident. A dry road, but there might have been a patch of ice. They didn't suffer. It was all over very quickly. Though that wasn't true: she found out later that her mother had died only after the paramedics had arrived. She'd been alive long enough to tell them that she'd seen the man driving the truck.

Hella sat back, thinking, her gaze turned towards the reddish glare of the midnight sun outside her window. A man, her mother had said. Not a boy.

And there was one other thing: the inspector had told her that there were no fingerprints on the steering wheel of the truck, that the driver had either wiped it or worn gloves.

She hadn't given it much thought at the time – she was a child – but now she wanted to slap herself. If she hadn't been so paralysed with fear and survivor guilt, if she'd been able to think straight about her family's deaths, she would have seen it much earlier.

Men who go around stealing logging trucks in the middle of April don't usually wear gloves. They neither know nor care about fingerprints – they're not that savvy. Unless they had already decided what the truck was going to be used for. Unless they were professionals.

17

There was a heaped plate of Karelian *piirakkas* on Jokela's desk, right next to a biggish mug of coffee. He pushed the plate of savoury pastries towards Hella. "Want some?"

"No thank you." She had woken up feeling nauseous, like the day her family had died. Maybe there was some logic in that, though she couldn't understand it. She dropped the typed report on Jokela's desk. "I'll leave you to your breakfast. Read it when you have time."

"Wait," he said, through the pie. "Just wait a second." He swallowed, took a sip of coffee. "So, what did you find?"

"Nothing. Johannes Heikkinen seems to be a perfectly upstanding citizen, and a completely normal one at that."

"Nothing?" Jokela picked up another *piirakka* and started spreading egg butter on it. "At all?"

"You sound surprised," Hella said. "Given the information you shared with me last time we met, I expected you to be relieved. Is there something I should know? Something I should have found?"

Jokela chewed thoughtfully. "Have you ever hunted crows?"

"No. And I hope I never will."

"They're intelligent birds. Very sneaky, too. Some folks

say it's a bit like hunting ducks, but it's not like that at all. Ducks are stupid."

"Right," Hella said. "Are you telling me this because you think Mr Heikkinen is a crow?"

Jokela pondered that. "Well, he's certainly not a duck. Anyway. To shoot crows, you first need to find out where they gather – that's easy enough, local farmers can tell you that – then you arrive there at daybreak, dressed in full camouflage, including a face mask."

"Because, being intelligent and sneaky, the crows can spot you from far away?" Hella thought of the polka-dot dress, her own inadequate camouflage.

"That's it. Then, you need something to attract them – an old fox pelt, say – and you need to let out a rallying cry. Caw-caw-caw. And then —"

"Thank you," Hella said. "I get the picture. Tell me about Heikkinen."

"I don't know what sort of animal he is, to be frank." Jokela sighed. "But you were right to suspect that I've been hiding things from you. There is something." He fumbled in his pocket, pulled out a small key that he used to unlock a drawer in his desk. "Here." He held out a slim paper file. "We've received three anony-mous letters. They started coming almost as soon as we approached him about the position. Strange letters, too. See for yourself."

Hella opened the file.

The letters were composed in blue ink on white office paper, the lines so straight that whoever had sent them must have used the ruled sheet as a guide. They were addressed *To the Head of the Homicide Squad.* "That's still me," Jokela said. "Interim Head." The handwriting was small and upright, with the *t*'s crossed low and short and outsize loops on the *d*'s. As for the content of the letters, the text was identical in all three:

> May I suggest that before you appoint Mr Heikkinen you look into his past? After all, it would be a pity to entrust the city's criminal police to a man who committed murder.
>
> Signed: A well-wisher

"Probably a malicious prank." Jokela grimaced with distaste. "But we have to check. That's where you come in. We can't hire him before we identify who sent these, and if there's something in Heikkinen's past that would make him unsuitable we have to know."

"And you couldn't have told me that from the beginning?" Hella asked. "Why?"

"I thought it was important for you to keep an open mind. You've met the people who know him best, and this sort of letter – well, this sort of letter usually comes from those nearest and dearest. So, who do you think wrote these?"

Hella thought. Not the neighbours, they wouldn't know about the appointment. Could it be Maria's sister or the mother-in-law? Given how they'd been gushing about Heikkinen, it seemed unlikely. "The cousin?" she said. "Veikko Aalto hates his guts. Or it could be someone from the SUPO, they'd be the first to know about the move, I suppose." Hella shook her head. "I don't know. These letters aren't specific. Besides, the identity of the person who sent them isn't so important. What matters is whether Heikkinen did indeed kill someone. His wife?" She glanced at Jokela. "Or could it be about something else? I don't know what sort of work he did for the SUPO, but I'd imagine it could have involved murder."

88

"I don't mind that," Jokela said. "If he killed people on the job because he had to, that's not a problem at all. It's his private life I'm interested in."

"You mean his wife, then."

"Wife, or someone else," Jokela said. He jabbed the letters with his index finger. "Why can't they be more specific, I wonder?"

"I talked to Tom, and he's reasonably sure the wife's death was a suicide," Hella said slowly. "Do you mind if I keep one of the letters? They're all in the same hand." When Jokela nodded, she picked up a letter by its corner and slid it into an envelope, and then inside her handbag. "In the meantime, can I ask you something?"

Jokela put the file into his drawer again and turned the key. "I'm listening."

"When I went down to Archives, I asked to see my parents' file. We talked about it, remember? Well, it was empty. Do you have any idea what could have happened to it?"

"None at all," Jokela shook his head and glanced at his watch, but Hella was not easily stopped.

"Can you go and check?"

"Not now."

"Today?"

Jokela let out a long and discontented breath. "I'll try to, OK? I'll let you know." He opened another one of his desk drawers and pulled out a white envelope. "Here's your payment."

"Thank you." Hella stood up. "I'll be in touch soon. Oh, and by the way: what do you do with the crows? Once you've shot them?"

"Do?" Jokela seemed surprised. "Eat them, of course. They taste a bit like waterfowl and go very well with cranberry sauce."

18

This time, the package was waiting for her on the windowsill, stuck between two long-dead geraniums in matching pots. Hella noticed it as soon as she rounded the corner. Her heart skipped a beat, but she didn't feel surprised. Deep down, she'd been expecting it. She stopped, rummaged in her handbag and popped another *salmiakki* lozenge into her mouth. Maybe she should have spied on her own front door in order to catch her mysterious visitor. "Some tramp," Erkki had said. Certainly, the new parcel looked as lopsided and dirty as the previous one. Why her, though? And why now?

Hella glanced around: there was no one. The street was empty. Although she was tempted to leave the parcel where it was, she knew she'd spend the rest of the day thinking about it. And so, after carefully looking it over first, she picked it up and carried it inside. She snipped at the string with the scissors, wondering if the grey felt tissue would be inside – and it was. But this time, there were no numbers. Just text, handwritten in block capitals, addressed to *H.M.* Hella stared, mesmerized. The letter was in Russian.

НАМ НАДО УВИДЕТЬСЯ, ПОГОВОРИТЬ. ЗАВТРА НА ЦЕНТРАЛЬНОМ ВОКЗАЛЕ, В 6 ЧАСОВ, НА ПЕРВОЙ ПЛАТФОРМЕ. БУДЬТЕ ОСТОРОЖНЫ, СОЖГИТЕ ЭТО ПИСЬМО. НИКОМУ О НЕМ НЕ ГОВОРИТЕ.

Long-forgotten memories of classroom Russian – a teacher who smelled of mothballs and cheap filterless cigarettes, a poem by Pushkin she never managed to learn by heart – flashed through Hella's mind. She could still speak a little, but reading was a different matter altogether. It had been too long. Should she show the letter to someone who spoke better Russian than she did? She didn't *want* to show it to anyone, though. Her mysterious visitor definitely meant to keep it a secret; he must have a good reason for that. She glanced at the squat Cyrillic letters, dark against the grimy paper, and thought. There was a dictionary somewhere in the house, probably in her father's study. She stood still, unable to make up her mind. First the numbers, and now this. What was this, some sort of espionage plot? And why couldn't she live like everyone else, with her curtains open and her door unlocked, without the feeling of constantly being watched?

Once inside the study, she realized that her hands were trembling. Angry now, as much with herself for being scared as with the author of the note for scaring her, she pulled the fat leather-bound dictionary from the shelf, dislodging a cloud of dust. But it didn't help much. She couldn't find the first word, or the second. The third meant *to see each other*. "Right," she snorted. And the fourth? *To talk.* She set the letter aside, thinking. In the Russian language, words have to be conjugated, that much she remembered. Six cases, three genders, two numbers, three tenses. That knowledge alone was enough to induce a headache. Still, she couldn't show this letter to anybody. She had to figure out by herself what it meant. So, presumably someone wanted to see her in order to talk. When? Where? The next sentence was easy; she found the words straight away. *Tomorrow, Central Station, 6 o'clock.* A.m. or p.m.? she wondered. There was no indication. *First platform.* All right. The next three words she couldn't find, then there was a reference to *this letter.* Then another three words that could have meant anything: bring a gun? Don't call the police? The letter concluded with *Don't talk.*

Right, Hella thought, brushing grey dust off her sleeve. This couldn't possibly be about Heikkinen – she'd got the first parcel before she'd even been to see Jokela about the job – and if it was a new client, he'd found a very unusual way of communicating.

She'd go, of course, both at 6 a.m. and at 6 p.m., but how would they understand each other if he only spoke Russian?

Don't talk, the letter said. That probably meant *don't tell anyone.* Don't count on it, Hella thought grimly. She wasn't going to run into whatever trap they might have set for her without taking precautions. It was a pity she had argued with Steve – he spoke some Russian, which would have come in useful now, and he understood the risks she sometimes had to take. Hella glanced at the letter again. Six o'clock, tomorrow. Morning or evening, Central Station would be full. A frenzied rush of commuters, newspaper boys yelling, street sellers with their trays of *piirakka*; no one would pay attention to her. But that gave her an idea. Hella smoothed her hair, bit her lips to give them some colour. Then she ran out of the house and up the steps to the porch next door. She hoped he would be home, and he was.

"Hey there!" Erkki's hair was wet, like he'd stepped out of the shower. As soon as he saw her, his face broke into a big grin. "Good to see you. Come on in." He stepped aside, offering her a glimpse of a sunny room painted white all over, its only spot of colour a hanging basket of vines. "I was planning to brew some coffee. Want some?"

Hella shook her head. "Thanks, but not now. I just came by to say I got the note you left me the other day and…" She stalled. She hadn't thought this through. Politeness required that she ask him to dinner now, cook him something. The thought made her cringe. Erkki was looking at her, amused. She took a deep breath. "And if you want us to have dinner together, we could do so tomorrow. If that works for you. But not too early. What?"

There was a twitch to the corner of his mouth, as if he was trying, and failing, to suppress a smile. "It would be my greatest pleasure. What time?"

"Well," Hella said, "I have an appointment in Kluuvi at six, so how about seven thirty?"

"I can meet you in Kluuvi, if that's easier."

"No. Come by my house." She would leave the two parcels in the middle of the coffee table. That way, if something were to happen to her, Erkki would be able to tell the police she'd gone to the appointment. She squinted up at him. "What did the tramp look like?"

"The tramp?"

"You said in your note that there was a vagabond trying to look through my windows, that you scared him away. What did he look like?"

"Tall. Taller than me, anyway. Grey." Erkki paused, thinking. "Bad teeth, pointy features, like he was famished. I got the impression he couldn't see much – he just kept blinking at me and mumbling something under his breath."

"And you haven't seen him since?"

"Well, I've been at work." Erkki shrugged. "No, I haven't seen him. Why? Is it important?"

"Probably not." Hella's voice trailed off. "Anyway. I'd better get going now. See you tomorrow."

"Sure. And don't worry, I'm keeping watch over your house. It's not a good thing for a woman to live alone. Besides, you can never be too careful with those Russians."

"What?" Hella whipped round.

"I said I'll watch over your place."

"No. The other thing. About him being a Russian. How did you know?"

Erkki grinned. "He called me *sobaka*. I don't speak Russian, but there was a family from Leningrad living next door to us when I was growing up. It was a long time ago, but I still remember what *sobaka* means. It means dog." Erkki glanced at Hella's porch, a few feet away. "And given how that guy said it, he didn't mean it in a good way either."

19

To a man with a hammer, it was once said, everything looks like nails. And what about a woman trying to solve a crime? A woman who heard the word *dog*?

Hella paused, her hand on the railing. What had the dog been called? Rekku? Haukku?

In her mind's eye, she saw the small fenced-in garden, the grass that hadn't been cut for too long, a small bed of yellow nasturtiums. The statue of a dog, almost life-sized, its mouth open in a snarl, looking ready to jump at Veikko Aalto. The dog's name was Tessu, she remembered that now. Hella glanced at her wristwatch. Would Mr Sopanen be home yet? She decided that it was worth a try.

To get anywhere in Helsinki, you either had to walk or take a tram. These had first appeared in the 1890s as horse-drawn single-track lines, before switching at the turn of the century to electric power. Now that the city was sprawling fast, the trams were losing ground in favour of cars, and the municipality had undertaken a massive renovation and extension of the lines that could no longer meet public demand. Soon, Hella thought, she'd have to invest in a car of her own. A second-hand Opel Kadett, perhaps, or a Soviet-made GAZ – something cheap, anyway. In the meantime, Puu-Vallila could still be reached by taking a northbound tram on the yellow line, then changing for the green. A long ride, but it gave Hella time to think about Veikko Aalto and about what he must have done. It was better than trying to come up with the reason why a Soviet vagabond wanted to have a secret meeting with her – and why he expected her to read, and speak, his language.

Afterwards, she could not remember having stepped off the tram, nor the short walk to Mr Sopanen's house on Virtaintie. Deep in thought, she only noticed her surroundings when she stopped under the green canopy of trees swaying in the gentle breeze and heard birds tweeting in the branches over her head.

As she had expected, Mr Sopanen was already home, though, like last time, he was still wearing a suit and tie. The children's toys had been cleared out of the hall, but the child itself was screaming somewhere out of sight – in anger or distress, Hella could not tell.

"Yes?" The man glanced up at her in annoyance. "Something you forgot to ask the last time around?"

"Actually, yes. It's about Tessu."

"What about Tessu?" The child's cries were getting stronger and more hiccupy.

"How did your dog die?"

"I told you. That man" – Mr Sopanen lifted his chin at the house next door – "fed Tessu something that looked like meat, and the poor thing died."

"No. I mean, what happened after Tessu swallowed the poison? Did your dog throw up, or scream in pain or —"

"Tessu just died. He just fell asleep and never woke up. That's all." The man balled his hands into fists. The screams coming from the house stopped for a moment, as if the

96

child was gathering force, then started again, a crescendo aiming for a perfect top G.

"Thank you," Hella said. "That was all." That was not all, but she doubted Mr Sopanen would be happy with what she had in mind. And given the screaming child, this was certainly not a good time to bring it up anyway. "Have a good evening, sir. Thank you for your help." Hella turned and almost ran, her heels clicking on the cobblestones. If she splurged on a taxi, with a bit of luck she could still make it to the Surgical Hospital before Tom called it a day and went home.

20

When Hella pushed open the door of his office, she saw Tom sitting with his head in his hands, a pair of round glasses she'd never seen before on the tip of his nose. The glasses flashed as he raised his gaze from whatever he was reading.

"Don't you knock?"

"Sorry." Hella slumped into the visitor's chair before picking up a leaflet for an upcoming seminar on fungal pathology, mycology and virology to fan herself. "Am I interrupting something?"

"Have you ever heard of John Gibbon and his wife Mary Hopkinson?" Tom took off his glasses and started polishing the lenses with his tie. "The inventors of the heart-lung machine?"

"No." Hella fidgeted in her seat, but she knew Tom wouldn't listen to her until he'd told her his story. "What's a heart-lung machine?"

"It's basically a mechanical lung, to support the circulation. The Gibbons spent a quarter of a century developing it. They tested the machine on stray cats that they lured off the streets with fish. In May 1935, they had a working prototype."

"Fantastic," Hella said. She didn't care one bit about the

Gibbons and their machine, but she knew when to keep her mouth shut. "So, what happened next?"

Tom smiled, like a little kid on Christmas morning. "It works on humans, can you imagine that? A month and a half ago, John Gibbon performed the first ever surgery on an open heart. He managed to repair an atrial septum defect in an eighteen-year-old girl" – Tom glanced down at the article he was reading – "an American named Cecilia Bavolek. He used an HLM and she survived. Can you imagine what this means for the medical profession?"

"A revolution," Hella said dutifully. It was all well and good, but Tom was a pathologist, so surely a dead body would interest him more? "Have you finished reading?"

Tom sighed. "OK, spit it out. What do you want me to do now? Stick your shoes in the freezer again, borrow a patient file?"

"Well…" Hella said, suddenly unsure of herself. Tom had helped her out before, that was true, but all that was small change compared to what she was about to ask him. "I need you to perform an autopsy. On someone who's been dead for a while. Actually, it's not even an autopsy, you won't need to cut it open or anything, all I need you to do is check for the presence of poison."

"Dead for how long?" Tom said.

"Five years. Give or take." Hella felt herself shrivelling under his stern stare. "And I'll help you dig it up."

"It?" Tom's eyes widened.

Hella braced herself and nodded. "Yes. It's a dog. You can… I mean, it's just a toxicology exam. I imagine you can autopsy a dog?"

Oxygen. Carbon. Hydrogen, nitrogen, calcium and phosphor. A little potassium, a tiny bit of sulphur and sodium. Gold. Chlorine. Magnesium.

"There's nothing to it," Hella said. She knew the basics, how after the heart stops, blood begins to pool in the lowest-lying areas of the body, rigor mortis sets in and eventually bacteria and chemical processes in the body start to break down tissue. "After five years, all that is left is dry skin, cartilage and bones: same for a dog as for a man. So, you can autopsy a dog, right?"

Wrong, apparently.

"I'm a doctor," Tom said, pulling a grimace. "Not a vet. Come *on*."

"It's a small dog. A Labrador." She added, unnecessarily, "Its name was Tessu."

"Labradors are not small." Tom rubbed his face with both hands. "Jesus, I can't believe we're even talking about this." He looked at her accusingly. "Where's this coming from, anyway?"

Hella lifted her chin. "I know that Heikkinen's mad cousin, Aalto, poisoned his neighbour's dog a week before Maria Heikkinen died. I'm no expert, but from the description, it sounds like a sleeping pill overdose. And when I was at Heikkinen's place, he mentioned that his cousin had seen his wife just hours before her death. You say she'd taken drugs, but maybe she was given them. We know she didn't have a prescription for pheno-barbital."

"And you think the cousin fed her the drug? Why?"

"I don't know," Hella admitted. "But when I interviewed Maria Heikkinen's mother, she said it was the cousin, Veikko Aalto, who first introduced her to her husband. They knew each other well, apparently. So maybe there's something there."

Tom loosened his collar with a finger and rolled back his shoulders. "So you think the cousin might have tested the drug on the animal first, and when he saw that it worked, killed the woman?"

"Yes. Do you understand now why I need your help to prove it?" Hella looked up at Tom hopefully, but he took a deep breath and shook his head.

"I can't do it." He held out a hand to silence her protests. "Not because I'm above digging up dog cadavers – it's not that. If that woman *was* killed, and I was too dumb to notice, now's the time to do something about it. But the thing is, Hella – it's like you said. After five years, all that remains is dry skin, cartilage and bones. There's no way I'll be able to find traces of sleeping pill abuse in *that*. Nobody can. I'm sorry, that's just the way it is. It's too late. If you want to prove it was murder, you'll need to find a different way to do it."

21

The morning dawned bright and beautiful. At five thirty, having gulped down a mug of bitter reheated coffee and run to catch a tram, Hella found herself passing under the vaulted art nouveau roof of Helsinki Central station, making her way towards the train shed that had no roof but plenty of seagulls circling overhead. It was too early for commuters and street vendors; she was alone. The station was waking up, the sculpted patterning on concrete pilasters turning from grey smudges to sharp angles, the spectacular chandeliers coming alight with reflected sunshine. It felt more like a cathedral than a railway station. Maybe that was suitable: a place where new life begins for some, where the journey ends for others.

She waited, thinking about the Heikkinen case because it was easier to focus on that than to think about her upcoming meeting. So, there was a chance that Veikko Aalto had killed Maria Heikkinen for some reason, drugged her with sleeping pills and left her passed out with a lit candle, home alone. Why? Out of spite? To punish his cousin, who had everything while he had nothing? She'd seen weaker motives than that. And as for Heikkinen, had he guessed what had happened? He must have had doubts. The fact that he didn't act on them could have been motivated by family loyalty, or lack of proof. Or maybe he thought no judge would sentence Aalto anyway, that his cousin's madness would protect him. Hella saw the house on Virtaintie, with its stink of decay and vermin running over the knick-knacks Aalto had hoarded as if there was a gaping void he needed to fill, as if by filling the house he could drive out his thoughts. She would speak to Jokela, ask if there was even the slimmest chance of a conviction. He'd probably tell her no, but she'd try anyway.

A teenager with a pillow crease on his cheek stopped a few paces away from her and leaned his bicycle against the wall. Its rear rack was loaded with newspapers tied neatly in bundles. Whistling, the boy pulled out the topmost bundle and settled it on his left arm; then he unfolded one of the copies so passers-by could see the headlines. WIND OF CHANGE TO THE EAST OF THE BORDER, the cover ran. STALIN'S LABOUR CAMPS: THOUSANDS OF POLITICAL PRISONERS MAKE THEIR WAY HOME.

The newsboy's timing was good: better than Hella's, anyway. Already, the station was filling up with people, and in the distance she could hear a train whistle. Then there was a burst of steam and the screech of brakes. The train arrived, a few minutes early.

Hella glanced at her watch: 5.56. By 6.01, her heart was hammering so loud, she was surprised the newspaper boy standing five feet away couldn't hear it. Would the vagabond come, or would he send someone for her? Or was he only a messenger himself? And if yes, who had sent him? She tried not to turn her head too much, but her eyes scanned the crowd, moving quickly from one passenger to the next. A small blonde woman struggling with a large hatbox and a toddler. A boy of about seventeen who had grown in length but not in width, as if he had simply been stretched. A man in a black overcoat – who on earth would wear an overcoat in the middle of summer, unless they had something to hide? The man stopped by the newsboy to buy *Helsingin Sanomat* and threw her an indifferent glance as he was waiting for his change. None of them seemed to take the slightest interest in her, although that didn't mean anything. She glanced at her watch. It was quarter past six. The platform was empty again; even the newspaper boy was gone. High above the tracks, a solitary seagull was making its rounds, its cries like fingernails scraping a blackboard. Hella shivered. Somehow, a space built to accommodate hundreds of people felt dead when those people were gone, as if it couldn't stand on its own, as if the blood had seeped out of it.

Maybe it was the echo. She heard the distant sound of a hammer landing on some metallic surface, then a patter of feet somewhere behind her back. She whipped round but there was no one, just the acoustics playing tricks on her. Her heart beat fast and loud. A sudden gust of wind blew a sheet of newsprint to her feet, Khrushchev's round peasant face smiling up at her from the page.

She had copied the numbers from the first parcel into her notebook, but this was a pure formality because by then she knew them by heart: *169062*. That didn't sound like a telephone number or railway locker code. Could it be some sort of cipher, where you replaced the numbers with letters and read backwards? It sounded unreal somehow, maybe because secret codes belonged in Edgar Allan Poe's novels or *The Adventures of Sherlock Holmes*. They had nothing to do with an exhausted PI who'd had another sleepless night and now needed more caffeine to keep on going.

Her thoughts drifted back to her interview with Johannes Heikkinen. As soon as she had confirmed she was Colonel Mauzer's daughter, he told her that her father was still a legend, that no one was up to his standard, not before and not since. That he had been the only one to oppose the Nazis they had been forced to deal with during the war. Heikkinen had obviously been trying to charm her, but Hella had to recognize against her will that it had worked. She had found Heikkinen sympathetic right from the start, because of his musician's hands and his beautiful well-kept home, though lots of people seemed sympathetic at first glance. By the end of the interview, she knew that she would have enjoyed staying longer. The realization was anything but comfortable: so she, too, could fall victim to a little flattery, like Aesop's proverbial crow?

She needed to see Heikkinen again, she needed to talk to him about his cousin. About the letters, too. Surely he knew something, and even if he didn't want to tell her about it, he might let something slip. She could do flattery, too, as long as it was part of her job. Then she'd go back to Jokela, and this time he would have to tell her what had happened to her parents' file.

It was half past six, and she was now almost sure the message meant p.m., not a.m. Still, she waited as the platform swelled with commuters again, then emptied, with cigarette butts and torn-up tickets the only proof of life. At 6.47, an old woman wearing a heavy padded gilet arrived with a broom. Hella shifted towards the ticket booth, pretending to be interested in the train timetable while the woman swept, then returned to her post. It was gone seven when she finally decided that she had waited long enough. She'd come again in the evening, maybe change her clothes too, make herself less conspicuous. The newspaper boy, who was back at his post, nodded at her as she walked by. Hella smiled back. She'd buy an evening edition tonight and watch the passers-by from behind her paper. Silly, a cliché, but perfectly suitable for someone who kept getting mysterious letters with secret codes.

22

"So how did your appointment in Kluuvi go?"

"Huh?" Hella glanced up at Erkki. He had already cleared his plate and was watching her, a grin playing on his lips. "Oh, that?" she said, through a mouthful of *kalakukko*, "Fine. Just fine."

That was a lie. She had spent the day at home, feeling increasingly jittery: sweeping the floor of the living room before abandoning the chore to peer outside from behind the curtains, compulsively surveying the quiet little street for anything that looked out of place. Making coffee and forgetting it on the stove until black smoke filled the room. Glancing out of the window again. Rereading the letter she'd received the previous night, checking the words one by one in the dictionary. Prowling her living room like a caged tiger while the minute hand of the wall clock crept slowly forward.

At five exactly, she had abandoned her broom next to the chimney and rushed upstairs to change into her polka-dot dress. It was only as she was locking the door behind her that she remembered her dinner with Erkki. She had planned to cook a meal for him, something simple, maybe a plate of smoked salmon with some boiled potatoes and a salad. But in her nervous excitement she had forgotten to stop at the grocer's, and now there was no time. They'd have to eat at the restaurant again. Hella decided that it didn't matter. What mattered was her upcoming appointment.

She had forced herself to only arrive at the station a few minutes before six, and to walk slowly. The newspaper boy was nowhere to be seen, but the station was as busy as expected, passengers rushing past with closed faces, train fumes turning the hot, acrid air grey. Instead of a newspaper, Hella bought another tin of *salmiakki* to give herself courage. Then she waited, refusing the temptation to glance at her wristwatch, her eyes scanning every face in the dense crowd of commuters heading back to their homes in the countryside. But, just like that morning, no one stopped to talk to her, and she didn't see the vagabond. She stayed long past the appointed hour, then had to rush back home so as to not be late for her meeting with Erkki.

When he showed up on her doorstep, she had bluntly told him that cooking was the last thing on her mind, and he hadn't said anything, just smiled and said that wasn't a problem, but she thought she'd seen a flash of displeasure in his gaze. He had taken her to a traditional Finnish restaurant that served food any decent housewife could prepare better at home.

Hella chewed thoughtfully on her *kalakukko*. The pie's crust was too thin, and even with a wrapping of bacon around it the small lake fish felt dry and brittle. Her mother had a better recipe. Hella remembered that she'd been planning to use it a lot once they'd bought the cabin by the lake, and would have done if she hadn't died by the roadside. Hella picked up her glass and took a swig, looking up at her date. Satisfied with her answer, Erkki hadn't asked any further questions, and instead was telling her about his day. Something about a new design for a transmission lever that was going to improve drivers' comfort. Hella stifled a yawn.

"I'm boring you."

"Not at all. I just didn't sleep well last night. Sorry. You were saying?"

He didn't need more encouragement. Hella had never imagined so much thought could go into a simple transmission lever. Then again, Erkki probably couldn't imagine how much thought could go into a simple note written in Russian and left under her door. She nodded, smiling, as Erkki did an impersonation of his boss, but her mind was on her no-show appointment. Steve would have asked, she thought. He would have wanted to know the details. He wouldn't have been satisfied with *fine* for an answer. She and Steve were over, though. It was no use getting all sentimental, thinking about how happy they could have been together.

"That's hilarious," she said.

Erkki stopped mid-sentence, frowning. Without a smile, he wasn't all that attractive. She noticed he had a chipped tooth. "Hilarious? What, the fact that I'm not allowed to perfect my invention?"

"No," Hella said. "Of course not." She felt herself blushing and raised her glass to her lips to stop herself from talking more nonsense. "Please go on."

"You're not interested, I can see that." He shook his head. "My fault – this kind of technical stuff isn't all that interesting to ladies."

What ladies? Hella thought. As far as she knew, all ladies were different and were interested in different things. Or was he talking about women like Mrs Vanhanen, with her poodle haircut and her Åland pancake? But she had already been caught not listening twice, and she was not going to add insult to injury and inform Erkki that there had always been groundbreaking women inventors: Josephine Cochrane, who invented the dishwasher, and Maria Beasley, who developed the modern life raft, Mary Anderson and her windscreen wipers and Melitta Bentz with her coffee filters and... and... Mary Hopkinson, the inventor of the heart-lung machine. Hella sighed and glanced at the dessert menu the waiter had placed in front of her with a flourish. If the food served in the restaurant was traditionally Finnish, the desserts were anything but: Bavarian torte, butterscotch cake and Parisian-sounding cherry macarons. It all sounded delicious ... and sickening, for some reason. She closed the menu and set it aside. "Nothing for me, thank you."

"No, have one," Erkki said. "I insist." He motioned to the waiter, ordering two macarons. "You're probably just tired because you work too much."

"Maybe." She smiled even though she didn't feel like doing so.

"Also, you've been drinking a bit more than a lady should. But I've been meaning to ask. Why would a girl like you decide to become a homicide detective?"

Hella stared into her glass, in search of a possible answer. Why would *anyone* want to become a homicide detective? The thrill of the chase, the excitement of outwitting cunning psychopaths, the unshakeable conviction of being a hero? The camaraderie of a squad room, the good wages, a generous retirement plan? She knew what everyone thought: that she'd become a cop because she had wanted to find her family's killer. Except that wasn't true. She had tried looking into her parents' case every now and then, in the hopes of finding something new, but that wasn't her biggest motivation. Until now, she had always believed their deaths to be an accident, a result of bad luck rather than human malice. After all, if her family had been wiped out by an earthquake or a tsunami, she wouldn't have become a seismologist. So why had she chosen that career?

She raised her eyes towards Erkki, wondering if he'd understand her explanation. "I guess it's about trying to restore order." She shrugged. "No, don't smirk. I'm not a very orderly person, my home's a mess, but that's different. It's just that – I need to know that the world makes sense. That people pay for the bad things they do. That actions have consequences. That's what the police are there for, restoring order to society." Hella looked away. "Sounds delusional, I know."

"Not at all." Suddenly, Erkki's hand was covering hers, and he was leaning forward. "I totally understand that. Many women are trying to make the world a better place. Schoolteachers. Nurses. It's because you care about the future your children will have."

"Maybe. Though I —" She glanced at the gloopy red pastry that the waiter had placed in front of her.

"Of course you do. You just chose a more difficult profession. I suppose it'll be hard for you to give it up once you're married, but maybe you could become a teacher instead?"

Hella glanced at him wordlessly – was that some kind of joke? – but Erkki was gazing at her with a sweet smile on his face, as if he'd said nothing wrong.

The room was full of shadows, the light cast by the midnight sun layered and blurry. The street outside, from what she could see, was empty – tree branches swaying in the wind, dark windows staring back at her, sparrows asleep on the power line. Hella took a step back, forcing herself to slow her breathing. No one. There was no one. And still she couldn't shake the feeling of being watched, like someone in the shadows had her in their sights, their finger on the trigger.

"You're an idiot, Hella Mauzer," she admonished herself out loud. In the empty room, her voice sounded harsh, unnatural, the voice of someone who had spent too much time alone. "Who would spy on you? The SUPO? You're not a threat to national security. Heikkinen?" But the package had arrived before she had even learned of the job. All this was ridiculous, the result of a woman gone half-mad from a lack of sleep, seeing danger everywhere.

Hella drew the curtains and lit the porcelain night light. It had been a long and unproductive day, where she had started working on a lot of things yet had accomplished nothing. Maria Heikkinen's death, for instance. Even though Tom had explained that a toxicology exam wasn't possible, Hella was still hoping to find some proof that Veikko Aalto had given phenobarbital to his neighbour's dog, and that he had later used the same sleeping pills on Maria. She couldn't think of a motive, either, but then again, what passed for a motive in a mentally deranged person's mind was anybody's guess. Hella stretched and yawned. She had planned to visit Maria's sister again in the afternoon, to try and find out more about the dead woman; but the day had passed in a flurry of anxiety, and then it was too late.

She pulled back the patchwork quilt and slid between the sheets, then, with a sigh, switched off the night light. Her thoughts were on the dead woman, who had gone to bed, just like her, and never woken up. How could she prove it was murder?

In every investigation, you come up with a lot of meaningless stuff. Things that might or might not be relevant.

Leads that seem promising at first then fizzle out in the end. Coincidences that turn out to be exactly that. Thrilling, pulse-racing insights that turn to dust when you take a closer look. A cliché, but you *are* looking for a needle, and the haystack is huge and forbidding. Sometimes, you only find it when the needle has already sliced the flesh of your thumb. And then you have to hope the needle isn't poisoned.

But at least in most cases you have *something* to go on. Here? Nothing. A long-dead woman, an autopsy that concluded the death was accidental, a drug that was easy to come by, a dead dog. An inconsolable widower and a string of anonymous letters. Sent by whom? Someone out to get Johannes Heikkinen, to make his life hell? Poison pen letters are the weapon of the weak. Those who know something yet are too afraid to tell. She needed to find the sender – it was as simple as that. Then she would know if she had anything on which to base her suspicions.

She was already drifting off, her thoughts slow and heavy, her breathing regular, when she heard it. Nothing more than a scrape, like someone moving a chair around. Or trying to open a window. She raised herself on one elbow, her eyes wide open, scanning the shadows. The sound was coming from downstairs. And then she heard a knock, like something small falling over. In less than a heartbeat, she was on her feet. Another heartbeat, and she had grabbed her gun and was charging downstairs.

"Don't move or I'll shoot."

She swept the room with her gun, and when she could detect no movement, fumbled for a light switch. The room blazed into light, empty. Hella let out a long, shaky breath. No one. There was no one. She cleared the kitchen and the hall, checking under the table, patting the old coats hanging from the rack. She must have been dreaming. Slowly, Hella made her way back upstairs and set her gun on the nightstand. Then she lay on her bed, forcing herself to breathe slowly, trying to calm the furious beating of her heart.

23

"Do you even know how to drive?" Steve asked, cocking his head at her. She'd woken him, Hella thought, even though it was already gone nine. His face was rumpled, his hair sticking out in all the wrong places; even his shirt was buttoned wrong.

As if he'd read her mind, Steve said, "It's Saturday," and yawned.

"I know. So can I borrow your car?"

Steve slanted an eyebrow. "You didn't answer my question."

"Of course I know how to drive!" Hella rolled her eyes. "I drove all the way from Lapland once!"

"Oh yes, there was that." He sounded unconvinced. "Look, give me ten minutes, and I'll take you. As long as we're back in Helsinki before three, that works."

Hella jabbed a finger into his shoulder, hard. "Chickened out, have you? I don't *need* you there. I don't *need* a driver. I can do this perfectly well myself."

"As you wish. Just remember that I've only just bought this car and that I'd rather get it back in one piece." He narrowed his eyes at her. "And you too, obviously." Steve sounded peeved, but he still reached out for a clothes rack and pulled the car keys out of a jacket pocket. "What's in Matalajärvi anyway?"

"Maria Heikkinen's sister has a lake cabin out there. I went up to see her this morning, but the neighbours told me she left for her weekend place. I want to talk to her again, and I want to get there before everyone is plastered on schnapps or whatever it is they drink. If I take a bus, it'll take *hours*."

Steve smiled. "And here I was, thinking you wanted to escape to the countryside for Juhannus. You know – collect seven flowers, put them under your pillow on Midsummer night, see your future fiancé in your dreams."

"I'd rather roll around naked in a wheat field," Hella grinned. "Get all the dew on me, become a sensational blonde."

"You are sensational. Not a blonde, of course, but who cares about blondes?" Steve looked her in the eye. "The reason I wanted to drive you? It's not because I don't trust you with my car, it's because I was hoping to spend some time with you. And also" – there was an amused twitch to his mouth – "I also wanted to be sure you're not going anywhere with that other guy. Erkki something or other. What if you spend a day with him and then accidentally see *him* in your dreams? I couldn't risk that, could I?"

Hella held out her hand. "Just give me the keys." She turned away before he could see that she was smiling too.

Finland is a land of a thousand lakes. That's what people say, but it's a gross understatement, because there are more than one hundred and eighty thousand lakes in Finland, dotted blue against the dark green of forests and rolling hills. Driving slowly on a winding road with water on either side of it, Hella thought that a couple of centuries back, there had probably been a lake for every person born in the country. Every Finn's dream was to own a small cabin by the water, a place for barbecues and long hours spent fishing, a place for celebrations like Midsummer. A place for families. Hella sighed. Did Steve think she'd just go to a cabin by the lake all on her own and daydream about a husband and a child? It wasn't an obligation to have a family; maybe she didn't feel like having one. Who was he to judge, anyway? Now the road curved gently between a tattered fringe of linden bushes, past a dilapidated barn and a henhouse, and through the open fields towards Lake Matalajärvi. She saw a family walking on the kerb, and slowed down. Two little kids in galoshes, and their parents, who seemed to be arguing, the man whipping round and pointing a finger in the woman's face. Hella passed them by at a crawl, her eyes on the road ahead, ignoring the kids' waves. Then, as soon as she had overtaken them, she sped up again. She wanted to be sure she'd make it to the Vanhanens' summer cabin well before eleven, when they would start setting the table and would have no choice but to invite her to eat lunch with them.

Matalajärvi was easy to find. It was a decent-sized lake set to the east of the much larger Lake Bodom, surrounded by a dense aspen forest that gave the Espoo province its name. Finding the Vanhanens' cabin, however, was a different story altogether: Hella had to stop at three different summer cabins, and interrupt two fishermen and an old man who was sanding a small wooden boat, before one of them finally pointed to the north.

"The family from Helsinki? That would be the third cabin down the road. Or maybe the fourth."

Hella ploughed on, hoping she wouldn't get stuck in a pothole. The trees knitted themselves above the narrow and winding path; it seemed as if the light of day had been wiped away, never to be seen again. By the time she got to the third cabin, after almost stalling in the dirt tracks, it was ten past eleven, and Liisa Vanhanen was crouched by the lake shore, washing tomatoes. A little further away, her mother was reclining on a lounger. Hella looked around. The Vanhanens' log cabin was tiny and greyed by the weather; with its low, moss-covered roof and its smallish windows, it looked like one of those Russian fairy-tale houses on chicken legs that might pick itself up and run at any moment. There was a sauna to its right, and a pier, where a man sat on an overturned bucket, his fishing rod gleaming in the morning sun. Mrs Vanhanen pressed a finger to her lips and Hella nodded, softly closing the car door. There were worse crimes than scaring away fish, but clearly not in Mr Vanhanen's eyes.

"What do you want?" the woman hissed. Her mother remained on the lounger, at a distance, but now she was leaning on her elbow, her sharp little eyes trained on Hella.

"I'd like to talk to you." Hella smiled ruefully. "Look, I'm sorry to barge in on you like this, but I needed to ask you something important. And I brought *mesimarja* to drink."

The woman looked at her, unsmiling. "Take it into the kitchen. And wash your hands. We'll be eating in fifteen minutes, and after that we can talk. You'll help me make *sauna vihtas*." She nodded at a heap of freshly cut birch twigs lying on the ground, waiting to be made into whips.

"All right," Hella said. "Let's do that."

She started towards the house, but the woman stopped her. "Don't tell him who you are. I'll say you're a friend of Maria's. He hasn't caught a single fish since daybreak, so now's not the time to talk to him about the SUPO, or about Johannes."

24

Mrs Vanhanen's husband seemed far more preoccupied by his lack of fish than by Hella's sudden appearance. "The women here," he said to her as he walked up from the pier, his round face glistening with sweat, a bottle of schnapps he had pulled from a wire holder set in lake water dripping all over his trousers, "they just keep…" He made a yappy mouth with one hand. "Can't stop, and of course the fish get scared. As they should." He stared balefully at the table piled high with food. "Is that all you've made?" His gaze skimmed the cucumbers and tomatoes cut up on a plate, the marinated herring buried under heaps of thinly sliced onion and its side of boiled new potatoes sprinkled with dill, the smoked salmon and the crusty rye bread before stopping on the dish of *vorschmack*. "You know I hate that stuff."

"*I* love it." Hella smiled defiantly. "It's delicious. My mother made it often." She turned to her hostess. "Do you add grated apple or onion?" Picking up a slice of bread, she started to spread the paste on it.

"Apple," Mrs Vanhanen murmured. "I use green ones."

Liisa Vanhanen's mother hadn't said a word since Hella showed up. Now she nodded slowly. "Apple, indeed. And you need two sorts of meat, beef and lamb. How did your mother make it?"

"Like this," Hella lied. She watched as Mr Vanhanen knocked back a glass of Terva schnapps filled to the brim. Not his first one, either – he was already swaying by the time he came to the table. Now he rose, slowly, and said, to no one in particular, "If this is it, I'll keep on fishing. Just make me a sandwich. And bring this." He pointed at the bottle, and then he was gone.

No one spoke for a while. Then Liisa Vanhanen exhaled slowly. "I'm sorry, Miss Mauzer. My husband works hard, he needs his quiet." She looked at the large back of the retreating man.

Her mother shook her head. "Johannes would have never behaved like that. Ever."

Liisa set her fork down with a bang. "I don't see what Johannes has to do with anything."

"He was a good husband to Maria."

"That's what you always said, yes." Liisa rose. "I'm going inside. I'll make us some coffee."

"I'll help you." Hella sprang to her feet. She stacked up the dirty plates and ran after her hostess towards the little cabin.

"Sorry it's a mess." Liisa pushed open the door with her hip. "You can put it here."

Hella dumped the plates on a small butcher's block. The walls of the cabin had been panelled in old pine, worn smooth with age and polish. The cabin was small and cramped, but it was cosy, too, with striped throws covering a bench and handwritten recipes pinned to the shiplap on the wall in the tiny kitchenette.

Liisa picked up a dish towel from the floor and folded it. "I keep meaning to sort things out, but there's also cooking to do, and Mother wants to talk all the time and…" She wiped her eyes with the back of her hand. "So, what did you want to talk to me about?"

"Veikko Aalto." Hella picked up a bundle of twine. "How about we get started on those birch whips while you tell me all about him?"

"Let me brew the coffee first." Her hostess reached up to a shelf, pulling down a tin of instant coffee. Then she switched on the gas ring under the kettle.

Hella used the time to peer at the recipes, written in big bold characters and heavily underlined. She didn't need to check against the anonymous letter in her handbag to know this was not the same handwriting. *Pulla* bread. Beef marinade. And here was the Åland pancake. A thought was tugging at her, like a needle stuck in the back of her mind, but no matter how hard she tried to grasp it, it evaded her.

"I don't know what I can tell you," Liisa Vanhanen said. "You've met him, right?"

"I have." Hella placed four cups on a round metal tray. "Is that a sugar bowl?" When her hostess nodded, she added it to the tray. "I'm asking because he seems to hold a grudge against Johannes Heikkinen. I was wondering if that was a recent development."

"No, he always hated his cousin. That's what I heard from Maria, anyway. It's been like that ever since they were boys, I don't know why."

"What about your sister?"

"Maria?" The woman grew pensive. "Maria got along with Veikko just fine. They were both dreamers. No practical sense at all, if you see what I mean." She put the coffee pot on a tray. "Let's carry that outside. Then you can help me with those birch twigs."

Hella waited while Liisa filled one of the cups with coffee and carried it to the lounger where her mother sat, looking angry. The heap of birch twigs smelled like childhood. Hella had loved making *sauna vihtas* when she was little, because she used them to chase after her screaming sister. But she hadn't made a birch whip in eleven years, and at first her fingers were slow and clumsy as she wrapped the twine around the branches, tying them together.

"The other day, your mother mentioned that Veikko was the one who introduced Maria and Johannes."

"They were in the same year at school." Liisa glanced at her mother. "They even went out together for a while, but that was before Maria met Johannes."

Hella tied the knot on the *vihta*. Could this explain why Veikko had murdered Maria? He might have thought she belonged to him, but then why hadn't he punished her earlier? Why wait all that time? She thought about the woman in the photograph Heikkinen had shown her. Maria had looked sweet and quiet, not the sort of person to ignite homicidal rage. Hella picked up another birch twig. "But they stayed friends? I heard he was with your sister the evening she died."

Liisa Vanhanen looked at her. "It wasn't what you think."

"Oh, I don't think anything at all. I was just wondering what Maria was like."

Liisa Vanhanen sighed. "My sister was unhappy, Miss Mauzer. She had a beautiful home and a caring husband, but she was still deeply, heartbreakingly unhappy. And we all refused to see it, we refused to help her, and now she's dead."

25

A mosquito landed on her naked arm. Hella slapped it, missed, heard the insect circle in a whiny buzz. The afternoon air was full of them, a high-pitched bloodthirsty army preparing its descent onto human flesh. Mosquitoes and sunburn, that's the Finnish summer for you, Hella thought, rubbing her elbow. She should have worn a cardigan.

She threw her sauna whip onto the car's passenger seat, together with her hat and a bouquet for Juhannus spells that Liisa Vanhanen had given her when she learned that Hella was single. "You'll see your future fiancé in your dreams," she said. "Just put it under your pillow." The seven flowers, her hostess assured her, each came from a different meadow. It couldn't fail.

Grinning, Hella turned the key in the ignition. In the distance, she could see Liisa Vanhanen and her mother, heads close together, talking, while the radio played "Trouble in Mind" by Dinah Washington. Choice of the month for Steve's Music Hour, repeated ad nauseam every time Hella switched on her own radio. She smiled: so Steve had managed to follow her to the lake after all. *Trouble in mind, I'm blue, But I won't be blue always, 'Cause that sun is gonna shine in my back door someday...*

She looked at Liisa Vanhanen's husband, who was still on the pier. Judging from the furious muttered swearing she could hear every now and then, he still hadn't caught a single fish. Hella shivered. She was glad she was able to leave before he called it a day and started punishing everyone present for his lack of success. *Trouble in Mind*, indeed.

Hella steered the car from under the trees and down the potholed dirt road, dissatisfaction gnawing at her like an itch. Detective work was mostly legwork, exploring avenues that led nowhere, talking to people who didn't know anything. She had spent over three hours with Liisa Vanhanen, yet she still hadn't learned much. The more they talked about Maria, the more she seemed like a catalogue item, a sketch of a woman – meek, dreamy, clumsy – rather than a real, flesh-and-blood person. Enough of a cliché to make Hella wonder if she had the full picture. She wondered if she should have told Liisa Vanhanen that, in all likelihood, her sister had been murdered. But what good would that have done? It wasn't like she could *prove* anything, or bring the suspect to trial. Hella shook her head and glanced in the rear-view mirror. By then, she had left the dirt road behind and was driving on an asphalt one that was just as narrow and winding. There was a forest either side of her, trees rustling like living things, green fingers swiping the car roof. The forest hadn't changed all that much since the time when there were more lakes in Finland than people. It had seen savagery and bloodshed, and it had kept on growing, unperturbed. Hella cursed under her breath. She couldn't do the same, couldn't let a crime go unpunished. But what *could* she do? What could one do if there was no proof, no formal police investigation, and no confession? What could she do if no one seemed to care?

She cared, though, maybe because there was another long-forgotten accident that might have been a crime. It was pure superstition, Hella knew that, but if she solved one, maybe, just maybe, she could solve the other? And she wasn't the only one who cared, either. Johannes Heikkinen spoke about his wife as if she was still alive. He had tried to save her, had been badly hurt in the fire. She needed to talk to him, tell him what she'd discovered about the dog, ask him if there was anything else he could remember about his cousin. At the very least, he'd be forewarned. Hella glanced at her wristwatch. If she wasn't delayed by traffic, she'd be back in Helsinki early enough to pay him a visit. That would put her mind at rest.

Deep in thought, she didn't notice the truck behind her until it was looming in her rear-view mirror. An outsize Volvo monster splashed with dirt, the front bumper rusty and crooked. Next to it, the small Opel looked like a gerbil chased by a mean cat. Hella edged closer to the side of the road, but it was too narrow and the big truck couldn't overtake her. She pressed hard on the accelerator, her heart pounding. She hated narrow country lanes, she hated the blinding sun, she hated the revving engine behind her.

The road made another sharp turn, and Hella clutched the steering wheel. And that was when she saw the child. He was wearing grubby overalls and a bucket hat, and he was standing still on the roadside. Hella threw herself on the wheel at the same time as her foot hit the brake pedal. The car spun; she gritted her teeth and closed her eyes, bracing for impact. The world fractured, as if in a kaleidoscope, before recomposing itself with a snap. Then, there was silence. She opened her eyes a fraction. Her car had stopped in the middle of the road. The truck was nowhere to be seen. The child was gone.

Slowly, Hella released her grip on the steering wheel. Her fingers hurt, and there was something dripping along the left side of her face. She raised her hand and touched it. Blood. Coming from a cut on her forehead. She must have hit her head on the window. That was strange, because she had no recollection of having been hurt. She looked around. At least she hadn't hit anything with the car. It could have been so much worse.

"What are you, mad?" A man was tugging at the car door, his face contorted in fury. "Don't drive if you don't know how to. Don't you have a husband?" He finally managed to yank open the car door, and Hella stumbled out into the summer air that smelled of warm pine needles and wild flowers. "Where's the boy?" she said.

The truck driver kept staring at her as if she was insane. "What boy?"

"There was a child here." Hella forced herself to enunciate the words slowly and carefully even though her head was splitting with pain. "Right here, by the side of the road." She pointed at the ground, which was covered with reindeer moss and blueberry leaves. "A young boy, maybe eight or nine —"

The driver shook his head. "There was no boy. Are you drunk?"

Ignoring him, Hella ran further down the road, on the lookout for the child. "Hey!" she cried out. "Where are you? It's all right."

The truck driver shook his head and crossed his arms. "There was no one there. You're mad, lady."

Hella looked around, stifling a sob. He was right. There was no child. Just an aspen, its trembling leaves dappled with sunlight, and an old barrow that someone had left by the roadside.

The driver was already turning away, muttering something about how dangerous women drivers were to the world. Hella watched as he made his way towards the truck that was stopped further down the road and climbed into the cabin. Once the Volvo was gone, she wiped the blood off her face with the hem of her skirt and got into her car. She waited for the shaking in her hands to subside, then she turned the key in the ignition. Much to her surprise, the engine started. She put the car into gear and began her long, slow way back to Helsinki.

26

Hella didn't start crying until she'd parked the car next to Steve's house and engaged the handbrake. She hadn't cried for years, and it felt strange, as if the burning sensation in her eyes and the tears belonged to someone else, someone who was weak and feminine and easily scared. She pressed her knuckles hard against her eyes to push back the tears, but still they kept coming, bitter and hot and angry. Mostly, she was furious with herself. How could she have made a mistake like that, how could she have seen a broken wheelbarrow and imagined a child? She had put herself, and the truck driver, in danger. And she hadn't even been drinking. Hella pinched the skin between her thumb and index finger, forcing herself to breathe slowly. She knew why it had happened, of course. While she was driving, a part of her mind had been running on a parallel track, travelling with her parents and Christina and Matti on that deadly April road. Anticipating the impact. She sniffed and bit down hard on her lip. At last her technique worked, and she stopped crying.

She wiped her eyes and stretched her neck to check herself in the rear-view mirror. Her face looked like she'd painted it with camouflage: streaks of dirt, smudges of dried blood, damp hair plastered across her cheeks. "You're a mess, Hella Mauzer," she said out loud. "Maybe you're not fit for this work any more. Maybe you'll never be until you manage to put your family's murder to rest." She fumbled for a handkerchief in her handbag, then spat on it and started rubbing at the dirt and blood on her face. Was that why her father had opted for early retirement? she wondered. Because he couldn't deal with the pressure that came with his work any longer? Because living on the edge, leaving his family for months at a time, keeping secrets that could challenge the status quo and cause governments to fall, was suddenly more than he could bear? Did he realize that all he wanted was to go fishing with his pal Kyander, a little log cabin of his own, a bottle of beer inside a wire holder set below the surface of an icy lake? Did you simply reach a point in life where, even though you were good at your job, you didn't want to do it any more?

Hella cast her mind back to the months preceding her family's deaths. Her father had always been a reassuring presence in her life, someone she could count on, someone who could make her laugh – and make her think. Though maybe that last part wasn't true. Certainly, she had never given much thought to his retirement. To an eighteen-year-old girl, any man over fifty was an antiquity, only good for spending his days in a rocking chair with a throw covering his knees, but her father hadn't been that old when he made his decision to retire. It was right in the middle of the Continuation War, when so much was at stake. Eager to recover territories lost to the Soviet Union, Finland had found herself embroiled in a bitter war, with the Nazis her unwanted allies. Tensions were running high. The Finnish government tried to retain its autonomy, but the Nazis wanted things to be done their own way, and sometimes it was hard to resist. Had her father left because he didn't want to take part in the Nazis' atrocities? Hella put the handkerchief away and pressed her fingers to her temples, trying to focus. Eleven years ago, she hadn't paid much attention to what the adults were saying, but her father's retirement had been big news. Her mother was speechless when he told her about it, that much Hella could recall. Still, as far as she remembered, they never talked about it. Her father just came home one day and told them he had put in his papers. That he was done with Suursaari and that he thought he had done the right thing. That was it. And then, a few days later, he told them about the cabin. And then they were all dead.

Maybe there was something in it, a reason behind his retirement that she hadn't thought to explore. Hella weighed her options. The SUPO wouldn't tell, of course. They'd hide behind some regulation or other, or tell her Colonel Mauzer's career was protected by the secret service's statute of limitations. It meant that, much as she squirmed at the idea, she had no choice but to go and see Kyander. If there was one man who could tell her the truth, it was him. The question was whether he'd want to. Hella glanced at her watch. She had been planning to see Heikkinen, and Kyander lived close to him, but the road back to Helsinki had taken much longer than expected, and now it was too late to see anyone. Especially given the state she was in. What she needed was a warm bath, and a bed. Hella got out of the car, locked it, then walked a few paces to Steve's house and slid the key into his letterbox, praying that he was still out and wouldn't rush to open the door.

Then she started to walk home. It was another beautiful evening, and the streets were teeming with people: elderly couples out for a stroll, families with toddlers in tow, dog walkers, teenagers in love. They all cast curious glances at her – apparently she hadn't done a good job of wiping the mess off her face, or maybe they could see the dark spots of blood on her dress. Hella walked quickly, trying to pretend she was ignoring them, just a woman going for a stroll, single but content with her life, thank you very much.

She preferred not to imagine what they thought of her – certainly nothing good. But it didn't matter. As she walked, she thought of Liisa Vanhanen, trembling before her bully of a husband, of her sister Maria, who everyone had thought was leading a good life until she was murdered, of all the women who had done nothing with their lives because they were too afraid.

Once she was back inside the house, Hella took off her hat and tossed it on the coffee table. She slipped her feet out of her shoes. It had been a long day. She knew she needed to wash her dress, but suddenly that seemed like more than she could bear. She stopped next to the washbasin and splashed cold water on her face. Then she made her way upstairs and sank into bed with the sigh of someone who expects a good night's rest. And it was good – until four in the morning, when Hella was woken by a loud knocking on her door.

27

At first, she thought she was dreaming again. When at last she climbed out of bed, stumbled downstairs and opened her door on the chain, she expected to find Steve standing on her doorstep. Or her neighbour, Erkki. What she didn't expect was a letter from Heikkinen, asking her to come at once.

"I'll drive you," the messenger said, gesturing towards an old Trabant waiting on the kerb. The messenger was young, almost a boy, with a prominent Adam's apple and his hair sticking up in all the wrong places.

"What happened?" Hella asked. She looked around for her hat, found it on the coffee table. Her handbag was right next to it.

"No idea." The messenger shrugged, opening the passenger door.

They rode quickly, and in silence. Ten minutes later, she climbed out of the car in front of Heikkinen's apartment building.

"My goodness, what happened to you?" Heikkinen stepped forward, his outline dark against the rising sun. "Is that blood on your collar?" Hella raised a hand to her temple, where the cut still throbbed. "Did someone *hit* you?" Johannes Heikkinen was watching her face, concern wrinkling his forehead.

Hella attempted a laugh. "I'm fine, thank you very much. Would you mind telling me why you called for me? The young man you sent wouldn't tell me anything, just kept repeating that my presence was required and" – Hella glanced over her shoulder, but the road was empty, the messenger already gone – "and so in the end I came, but now I'd like to know what…" She narrowed her eyes at Heikkinen. "Is this about your cousin?"

He let out a long sigh. "Yes. Jesus." He ran a hand over his face and Hella saw that his eyes were bloodshot and full of tears. "This is really terrible. I was asleep when I heard footsteps – I'm a light sleeper – and so I grabbed my service weapon and opened the door a crack. The curtains were drawn. All I could see was the silhouette of someone coming up the stairs, holding what looked like a club, or a shotgun with the barrel sawed off. I took aim, and then I said: *Don't move or I'll shoot.*" Heikkinen's mouth twisted like he'd tasted something foul. In the narrow entry hall, he was standing too close and Hella could see the silvery stubble on his chin and the hollow between his collarbones where his pulse was beating.

"But your cousin didn't stop," she said. It wasn't a question, because she thought she already knew what must have happened.

Heikkinen shook his head with a bitter smile. "No, he didn't. Didn't say anything either. If only I had known it was him…"

"Did you shoot?" Hella asked.

"I did. Missed him, thank God for small mercies. But the shot must have startled him." Heikkinen nervously paused, then, making a visible effort, looked her in the eye. "You know, I can still see it, in slow motion. If I'd been quicker, I could have grabbed him – he was that close. But I didn't. I didn't. And so Veikko fell backwards on the stairs and broke his neck. He's... There's no pulse."

"I'm sorry," Hella said. Nothing came to mind but platitudes, and Heikkinen probably didn't care about those. "It must have been a shock."

The man continued as if he hadn't heard her. "I thought it was a burglar. I was *sure* it was a burglar. Even when I switched on the light, I still didn't recognize him. He was lying in a heap at the bottom of the stairs, all elbows and sharp angles and dirty clothes, and at first I thought I'd leave him there, let the police deal with the mess. But then I started wondering if maybe he was still alive, if he needed help, so I turned him over." Heikkinen closed his eyes and swallowed. "It was my cousin. On the rug. At the bottom of the stairs. And he was dead."

"I'm sorry," Hella said again. She laid a hand on his sleeve. "Is he still in there?"

Heikkinen covered his mouth with a fist, averting his eyes as he fought for control. Then he nodded towards the living room. "At the bottom of the stairs. I wanted to pick him up, make him comfortable – ridiculous, of course, but there it is – and then I remembered you should never touch a dead body before the police have seen it, so I left him there." The corner of Heikkinen's mouth curled downwards. He still wouldn't meet her eye. "I suppose that for a man who expected to head the homicide squad, I don't have all the right instincts."

Hella wondered if that was the reason he'd called her. Or could there be something else there? She tried to sneak a glance at the door, to see if the lock had been jimmied. Heikkinen had been waiting for her with his back to it when she arrived, so she hadn't seen anything. Or had he woken her in the middle of the night because he needed help trying to figure out what to say to the police? Because he was afraid his appointment wouldn't be confirmed? As if reading her thoughts, Heikkinen said: "I'm not afraid of the consequences, you know. But what people think of me – it matters. Probably more than it should." He ran a hand through his hair. "Do you want to see him?"

And do what? Hella thought. I can't revive the dead. And I'm not the police or the pathologist. She knew she should refuse, so she was surprised when she heard herself reply, "Of course." Heikkinen breathed a sigh of relief and nodded. She followed him to the expensively appointed room in which they had chatted over coffee just two days ago. Now the heavy silk curtains were drawn against the night, and the air smelled of excrement and fear.

Heikkinen stopped at the door, seemingly unable to take a further step. Hella brushed past him. Veikko Aalto was lying on his back, his neck twisted at an unnatural angle, his mouth half-open, a trail of darkened blood running from his nose. The orange cat was next to him, sniffing his hair; it slunk away as Hella approached. Aalto was dead all right, but he looked like he was laughing, the blue eyes crinkled, a bronze chandelier reflected in his pupils.

Almost despite herself, Hella went through the check-list that had been drilled into her by years of practice. No bruises or visible wounds, except for the nosebleed. Clothes dirty but intact. No smell of alcohol she could discern, though with the stink of the inadequately washed body and the fact that the dead man's sphincters must have loosened, it was hard to be certain. The angle of the neck looked consistent with a fall down the stairs. No sign of a struggle. She straightened up, her gaze running past the fireplace, past the little straight-backed chair where she herself had sat the other day, and stopping on Heikkinen.

"If you haven't already done so, now is the time to call the police."

"Of course," Heikkinen said, flustered. "Please sit down." Hella watched as he picked up the telephone and after waiting for the connection to be put through talked to the officer on duty. "Oh yes," Heikkinen was saying. "Yes, I'm absolutely certain he's not breathing. Yes, of course, if you need to send a doctor to be absolutely sure."

And there goes Tom's beauty sleep too, Hella thought. He'd be surprised to find her here, and not exactly delighted. *What sort of a woman are you, Hella Mauzer,* he would say, *if you can't keep out of trouble?* In the background, Johannes Heikkinen was still talking, giving someone directions. Hella looked at the dead body by the stairs again, wondering why Veikko Aalto had come to his cousin's house in the middle of the night. She'd probably never know now. Heikkinen finally hung up, and she was turning towards him to say something when out of the corner of her eye she caught sight of something yellow peeking out from under the tassel-trimmed belly of a recliner chair.

"They promised they'll be here soon," Heikkinen said, his voice high and surprised. "Twenty minutes at most. What is… What did you find?"

Hella, who had dropped to her knees, was still staring at the object under the chair. Pale yellow, heavy and smooth, liquid inside. If she'd had a pair of gloves, she could unscrew the cap, sniff the contents, but she didn't need to check to be sure. "I think I know what your cousin was doing here," she said. "Assuming that's not yours."

136

Heikkinen shook his head vehemently. "Never seen it in my life. What is it? Could it be…" Suddenly, his eyes widened. "Don't tell me it's —"

"Yes." Hella nodded. "It's petrol. The can is full of it."

28

The rising sun looked like a planet on fire. Hella stood by the window, watching the gauzy clouds drift across the morning star's furious glare, thinking about accidents. Her hands were clasped around a steaming cup of coffee that Heikkinen had made for her.

She hadn't expected the police to arrive so fast. Seventeen minutes after Heikkinen had hung up, there had been a knock on the front door, and Hella saw her old colleague Inspector Pinchus stoop as he crossed the threshold. He nodded curtly at her. "Miss Mauzer. Always a pleasure." Rubbing his hands together, Pinchus angled his long neck like a heron about to gobble up a small fish. "This city probably sees one homicide a year, and you just happen to be there every time it happens."

Heikkinen threw his hands up in the air. "It was *not* homicide. Would you please tell him, Miss Mauzer."

Hella told him. Or, rather, she repeated what Heikkinen had told her, and pointed at the can of petrol she had found.

"Malicious intent, huh?" Pinchus said. "Let's see that." He circled the body, tut-tutting, a gloomy smile playing on his lips. "I see the lock has been forced. These buildings are all the same, they look splendid on the outside but the locks are standard pre-war and can be opened with a hairpin. And I assume you didn't draw the bolt. Rather careless of you." He knelt by the body. "So, tell me, Mr Heikkinen, did your cousin really hate you that much?" Somehow, Pinchus always managed to make every one of his questions sound like an accusation.

"I'm afraid that was indeed the case, officer." Heikkinen crossed his arms over his chest. "Will the pathologist be coming as well?"

"Oh, yes," Pinchus chuckled. "Another old friend." He pointed a long index finger at Hella. "Your pal Räikkönen. I'm surprised you didn't call him yourself."

"That wasn't my role," Hella said. "I understand you must be upset at having been woken at —" She didn't have time to finish her sentence, because Tom burst into the room, very much his usual cheery self. Even at this hour, there was a carnation in his buttonhole. He, too, arched an eyebrow when he saw Hella.

"I was told there was a mortal struggle here, but no one informed me it involved *you*. That dress looks like it's been in a fight and lost. And your face…"

Hella shrugged. "This isn't about me. I was in a minor car accident, that's all." She abstained from specifying that she'd caused the accident herself. "This man here" – she pointed at the body – "appears to have fallen down the stairs."

Tom had already knelt beside the corpse with an agility that was surprising in a man of his size and bulk. Next to him, Pinchus was still staring, eyebrows raised, his long mouth turned down at the corners.

"Do take your time, Dr Räikkönen. It's not like we ordinary folks have much to do at five in the morning." He glanced at his wristwatch. "Five twenty-two, actually."

Tom didn't answer, his big hands gentle as they moved over the dead body. Finally, after what seemed like an eternity, he rose, brushing imaginary dust from his trousers. "I can do a post-mortem later this morning," he said to Pinchus. "Feel free to come and watch."

Pinchus examined him critically. He had never liked Tom, but then again, he had never liked *anyone*. "Maybe I will," he said in a voice that showed such complete lack of enthusiasm that it made his presence at the autopsy sound unlikely. Then he turned to Heikkinen. "You said earlier that you fired a shot and missed. Can I see where the bullet lodged itself?"

"Of course." Johannes Heikkinen pointed towards the top of the staircase. "I was standing there, you see. The first door to the right is my bedroom. The bullet went into the window frame – you can see the impact over there."

Both Hella and Pinchus looked up. Up near the ceiling, Hella could just discern a small entry hole in the woodwork.

"Hmm," Pinchus muttered, as he started climbing the stairs.

Tom was already waving goodbye to Heikkinen. "I don't think you should blame yourself, sir. An unfortunate accident, happens more often than anyone thinks." And, to Hella: "Would you walk me out?" She followed him down the corridor. On the doorstep, he paused. "Did you tell this guy Heikkinen you thought his wife had been murdered by his cousin?"

Hella danced from foot to foot. "No. I was intending to, but I didn't get a chance. I'm wondering if I should tell him now. It would probably help to put his mind at rest."

"Hmm," Tom said, echoing Pinchus. Then he raised his hat to her and was gone.

. . .

Hella had stood by the window since Tom left, drinking coffee and watching the sun rise. Now she turned towards Heikkinen.

"Why do you think your cousin came here in the middle of the night, carrying a petrol can?"

"I should imagine that was obvious." Heikkinen looked at her angrily. "He certainly didn't come for a friendly chat by the fire. More likely, he planned to *start* a fire."

"Yes," Hella said, turning away from the window. "But why now?"

"How would I know?" Heikkinen's shoulders slumped. "You know, Veikko was such a cute boy as a child, and he had such a wild imagination. When we were growing up, everyone had been in thrall to him. But there's no doubt at all that, over the years, he grew strange. Moody. Sometimes violent. Still, he was family, so we all supported him as best we could. You know what they say about people like him, that he doesn't have all his marbles. That's not a good enough reason to ban a person from your life."

Hella set her empty cup on the coffee table, next to an overflowing ashtray. "What about your wife?"

"What about her?" Heikkinen stared.

"When we first met, you said that your cousin had been with Maria on the day of her death." Hella looked him in the eye. "So, I wondered how they got along?"

"They were friends. Very good friends." Heikkinen pulled a crumpled cigarette pack out of his pocket and lit up. "Very close, when they were younger. When she married me, they became more distant but still kept in contact."

"And you never thought..." Hella hesitated, unsure how to say it. "You never thought that Veikko might have been involved in her death somehow? Dr Räikkönen told me that Maria had a high concentration of both promethazine and phenobarbital in her blood. She had a prescription for one of those drugs but not the other."

Heikkinen took a drag on his cigarette. "You surely don't mean that —"

"Oh yes," Hella said. "I do mean that. There's no reason for you to know this, but your cousin Veikko fed sleeping pills to his neighbour's dog and the poor beast died. I checked the dates – that was barely a week before the fire broke out in your house. You really never thought he might have been involved?"

There was a long silence while Heikkinen watched the smoke trickle out of his cigarette. Then he sighed. "I did have my suspicions."

29

Outside, the street was waking up. Hella could hear the regular shush of a street sweeper's broom, a patter of children's feet, bicycle wheels gliding along the pavement. The sun was higher in the sky now, flooding the room, chasing away the night's shadows. She glanced at Heikkinen. His face was creased, dark circles under his eyes, mouth set in a grim, unyielding line.

"If you suspected your cousin, why didn't you ever say anything to the police?"

Heikkinen stubbed out his cigarette. "Because I was unable to. When I tried to save Maria, I inhaled quite a bit of smoke, and suffered burns on my back. The doctors sedated me. I spent weeks drifting in and out of sleep, and when I came to, when my head was finally clear, the inquest was over. Maria's death had been ruled an accident. Now, I'm no cop – even if I did once stupidly think I could run a homicide squad – and I'm not a pathologist. I thought that if it was murder, they would have seen it." He rubbed his face in his hands and massaged his temples as if he was starting with a headache. "If I'm honest, I probably lacked courage too, or maybe I let myself be guided by misplaced family loyalty. Even if you don't like them, you don't want to accuse your family without a good reason, and I had nothing but vague suspicions. I thought about it for a long time and in the end decided it was best not to say anything. After all, that wouldn't have brought Maria back, and my wife was the only one I cared about. Still, once I was out of the hospital, I asked Veikko to come over to my house and I asked him point blank if he'd done anything to hurt Maria. He denied all involvement. We argued. I haven't had much contact with him since." Heikkinen paused, then looked at her. "You know, if what you say is true, then I don't regret him being dead now. But I do regret having accidentally killed another human being."

"I understand."

Hella thought of Tom, who'd had doubts even back then but had still ruled Maria's death an accident. Of the SUPO, who suspected suicide but thought it best to give the poor woman a decent Christian funeral. Of Veikko Aalto's mad eyes and his house full of indescribable junk. "I suppose that makes sense." She glanced towards the top of the window frame, where the bullet had gone into the woodwork. "You still haven't told me why you wanted *me* to come here?"

Heikkinen looked down at his hands. "I suppose I wanted you to speak to Jokela. Given that you were investigating me and all. But it was a stupid idea." He glanced up at her. "I'll speak to him myself. Of course, he'll have to find someone else to lead the homicide squad."

"It was self-defence," Hella said. "There will be an investigation, but once that's over, I don't see why you can't still take the job. It doesn't make you" – she hesitated, looking for the right word – "doesn't make you any less qualified."

"Well, I wasn't very well qualified to begin with." Heikkinen rose to his feet. "I guess I'll just remain a drudge at the SUPO. Careers like the one your father had are few and far between. The rest of us are just cogs in a big, well-oiled bureaucratic machine. Nothing remotely mysterious or thrilling about what we do. Not any more."

Hella rose too. "And what is it you do, exactly? I never asked you."

"Internal affairs." Heikkinen snorted. "Mostly making sure my fellow officers don't stray and retain their fine moral character. Which was why I was amused at the thought that you were investigating *me*."

"Sounds fascinating," Hella said.

He laughed. "It's not. And, if you'll allow me, you're an unconvincing liar. But anyway." He held out a hand. "Thank you for coming. I am indebted to you. Any time you need help, just ask."

Hella thought about the night's events and shivered. "I'm sorry I didn't come to see you yesterday evening. I could have told you that I suspected your cousin. Maybe things would have turned out differently."

"Maybe," Heikkinen said. "Though I doubt it." He opened the door for her. "Try to get some sleep. You look exhausted."

"I'm going straight back to bed," Hella lied. "And then I'm going to wash this dress." She smiled. "It was nice meeting you. Even under these circumstances." She threw one last glance inside the apartment that now looked quiet and unthreatening. "And I'm sorry for your loss." She didn't specify which loss she meant, maybe because she wasn't sure about it herself. That of a cousin Heikkinen didn't care about? That of a long-dead spouse? Or the loss of his peace of mind, gone forever because he had killed a man?

Hella stood on the pavement, thinking. The city around her was fully awake now, men with briefcases rushing to work, housewives shopping for groceries, school-age children now out for the summer break. The air smelled of salt and diesel fumes, and seagulls circled overhead. Would Kyander be home? she wondered. Given the time of day, that didn't seem likely. But she was a street away, and she thought she'd give it a try.

She pulled a handkerchief out of her handbag, spat on it then started to rub at the bloodstains on her dress, but stopped when she realized she was only making things worse. Hella sighed, smoothing her hair, tucking it under her straw hat. So, she wouldn't be presentable. No matter. She had long since abandoned the hope of one day making a good impression on her father's oldest friend and closest associate. She lifted her chin high, pulled back her shoulders and started to walk towards Kyander's home.

30

The house was exactly as she remembered: egg-yolk yellow, with stuccoed columns supporting a massive porch, and a gravel path leading up to it. The shrubs bordering the path on either side were trimmed to perfection, the flower beds beyond luxuriant with nasturtiums. Before Hella had a chance to ring the bell, the door opened and she found herself facing the disapproving gaze of an elderly woman.

"I'm Miss Mauzer," Hella said breezily. "Could you please let Mr Kyander know I'm here?"

The woman kept staring, her thin lips pursed. She had gossamer-fine hair arranged in a bun, and a big hairy mole on her chin. Finally, she said: "I'm afraid Mr Kyander is not here, Miss."

"I can hear him," Hella protested. "Don't tell me he's not home, because I know he is."

The woman raised her eyebrows, as if scandalized that a girl in a rumpled dress would dare contradict her. "I'm telling you he is not —"

"Oh, hel-lo, my dear child!" Kyander exclaimed in a sing-song voice. "Let her in, let her in. My oldest and dearest friend's youngest daughter. Would you care to have breakfast with me?"

The housekeeper sighed and stood aside, her cold stare following Hella as she made her way to the breakfast room. "I've already had breakfast," Kyander was saying, "but I'll have a coffee with you. Would you like some fried eggs? My maid can fix that for you. Or maybe some pancakes with smetana?"

"I'm good," Hella said. She was hungry, but she wasn't going to eat in front of Kyander. He might pretend they were friends, but for her this wasn't a friendly visit. She sat down beside a round table covered in white embroidered cloth. "But I'd love a cup of coffee, thank you." While Kyander poured, she studied the family portraits that hung in heavy gilded frames and the collection of antique silver goblets decorating a sideboard. Kyander had inherited a lot of money, she knew that. And he had done well for himself.

"So what have you been up to?" Kyander asked, placing a cup before her. "Sugar?"

Hella dropped a lump into her coffee and stirred. "This and that," she said vaguely. "Mostly trying to sort out my father's things. I moved back into the family home."

Kyander shook his head, his bald patch gleaming in the light from the overhead chandelier he must have forgotten to switch off. "Lay the dead to rest," he said, "that's my advice, whether you want to or not. Nothing you do will bring them back. And most likely, you'll do more harm than good."

"I know that." Hella took a sip of her coffee. "That's what I'm trying to do, actually, turn the page. But there are some things that keep bothering me."

Kyander smiled, baring two rows of startlingly white and straight teeth that were very obviously false. "There will always be things that bother you. That's just the way you are. Always trying to read more into things. Now, I hope you will forgive me, but I think that comes from you not being married. If you had a husband and a child to think about, you'd spend less time inside your own head and more time in the kitchen." He cackled. "Don't get me wrong. I'm sure you're all right at what you do. But you're a woman, and all women want to marry and have babies." Kyander slurped his coffee. "Only natural, right?"

The patronizing bastard! Hella wanted to scream. A few years back, she'd have told him exactly what she thought, but she was older and wiser now and better able to keep her eyes on her goal. "Indeed," she said, and even managed a smile. "But you know how we ladies are – once we get something into our heads, it becomes difficult to think of anything else. I was hoping you could help me. Besides, when you said you were writing your memoirs…"

Kyander sighed. "Go ahead then, ask your questions." He was smiling, but his small eyes were watching her.

"It's about my father's retirement," Hella said. "You see, I'm wondering now why it was so sudden." She set down her coffee cup. "I remember he wasn't happy when our country had to tolerate the Nazis during the Continuation War, but I don't know what he was working on at that time. I wondered if that was significant." She made herself look him in the eye. "I was hoping you might be able to tell me what he was doing."

Kyander relaxed. She could practically see the tension seeping out of his shoulders. Whatever he hadn't wanted to tell her, it wasn't this. "Your father was mostly taking care of prisoners of war," Kyander said lightly. "Making sure there weren't any troublemakers, that things were running smoothly. At the time, we weren't structured as we are now, the responsibilities of each job weren't clearly defined. Everyone rolled up their sleeves and did what was

149

necessary." He lowered his voice confidentially. "If you want to know what I think, your father just got bored. We were at war with the Soviets. He couldn't go there any more, all he could do was watch from the sidelines. And then there was your nephew. What was his name, Olavi?"

"Matti," Hella said.

"That's right. I guess your father simply decided that it made no sense for him to keep on doing the work. That he'd be happier at home. I must admit the same thought crossed my mind too."

"But you didn't act on it," Hella said.

"No, I didn't. Toyed with the idea for a while, then decided that my country needed me."

That implied that her father had been selfish or unpatriotic to choose retirement. Hella gritted her teeth and went on questioning. "So nothing happened in the months or weeks leading up to his retirement that was even a little bit out of the ordinary? He just woke up one day and decided that he was no longer useful and that he didn't like his job all that much, is that it?"

"If you want to put it like that." Kyander sighed. "Your father was a really fine man, you know. You're being too hard on him. There's nothing wrong with wanting a little peace and quiet."

Hella reached for her coffee again, smiling sweetly. "You didn't answer my question. I asked whether anything unusual had happened."

"Not that I know of." Kyander frowned, affecting intense concentration. "He wasn't very keen on our German friends, not really cooperative, but then, they didn't ask him for much. That's it."

"He told me once that he'd had to take care of Russian refugees. Russian Jews. They were on some island in the

Baltic," Hella said slowly. "I remember he seemed unhappy about that. But he didn't mention any details."

Kyander shrugged. "A spy never tells. Your father spoke good Russian, he could communicate with those people. But that was hard on him, and maybe also he lost faith in himself. And when that happens…"

Although he left his sentence unfinished, the meaning was not lost on Hella. A spy who could no longer trust himself to do the right thing was no longer good at his job. And maybe Kyander was telling the truth, but she didn't want to believe him. Her father had not been like that.

Kyander looked at his watch. "Was there anything else you wanted to ask me?"

"No." Hella rose. "Thank you very much for your time." She glanced down at the table. "And for the coffee."

"Not at all, my dearest. I just hope that you'll listen to my advice and not spend any more time dwelling on the past. It's Midsummer night soon, and I don't know if you believe in everything they say, but maybe you'll see your fiancé in your dreams?"

"Maybe," Hella said. She turned to go, then stopped. "Have you chosen your fishing rod yet?"

"What?"

"Your fishing rod. For your lakeside cabin?"

"Oh, that!" Kyander exhaled a great bark of a laugh. "No, I need to get started on that. I've never been one for country living, you know, never been tempted to escape to the wilderness, but I guess that's what old age does to you."

"Right." The lobby seemed empty, but she could bet the housekeeper was spying on her from one of the many doorways that opened onto it. Hella shivered. Now she knew Kyander was lying, she couldn't wait to get out of that house. The very act of breathing hurt, as if the air inside the place was poisonous.

"Come back any time you feel like it," Kyander said.

"I will." Hella managed a smile that was as bright as it was fake. "I'll be back soon, I promise."

31

Hella sat on a bench by the Cholera Basin, watching the light shift by degrees as clouds moved in front of the sun. In the warm summer breeze, gulls hung stationary, like kites, and the air reverberated with children's joyful cries. She thought of the holidays she had spent with her parents as a little girl. The marshes where she picked cranberries, staining her fingers with blood-red juice, and the thick carpet of soft pine needles in her favourite hiding place behind a large rock, her mother's voice calling her name because dinner was ready. She recalled the silvery flash of the fish that her father pulled out of the water, the smell of coffee boiling on a gas ring and of sausages grilling over the fire. And she also thought about the calendar on her kitchen wall, the date of her family's death circled in black ink. She could still hear her father's voice in her ears: "Kyander's found us a perfect lakeside cabin. We'll buy it together – he loves fishing as much as I do. The seller said we can come and visit tomorrow, in the early afternoon. Kyander will come, too, so you'd better make a sandwich for him as well." Her mother had bought smoked salmon for the sandwiches, Hella remembered, and baked *pulla*. Then, the next morning, getting up at daybreak, she had prepared a big thermos of coffee.

Now, Hella wanted to kick herself. Kyander had set them up, that much was obvious. He had pulled out of the visit to the cabin, pretending he had urgent work to do. How could she have not seen it before? Was it because she had trusted her father's judgement to the point where she never questioned the motives of his best friend? Or was it precisely because she couldn't *see* a motive, even now? After all, why would Kyander want to kill her family? Her father was going into retirement, so he didn't represent a threat professionally. They hadn't argued – she would have heard about that, and besides, in that case, her father wouldn't have wanted to buy a cabin with him. There was no money at stake. No woman involved. Just long shadows on a winding country road, and the revving of a truck engine.

Hella had been sitting so still, for so long, that seagulls began to squabble at her feet. The more she thought about the reasons why Kyander might have wanted to murder her family, the less she could find any. Or maybe it had been nothing personal? At the time, Kyander had seemed greatly affected by her parents' deaths, but maybe she was mistaken on that too, maybe anyone whose words chimed with her own feelings and grief would have seemed sincere to her. The nebulous blur of her thoughts hardened until that was all she could think of. Had her father uncovered something he shouldn't have, and his employers decided to silence him? Had the rest of her family been collateral damage, because a hit-and-run accident would seem more natural to whoever had ordered it than the lonely death of a spy?

Flapping its wings, a seagull hopped onto the bench and threw an angry glance at her, as if she was somehow in the way. Hella shifted towards the edge of the seat. Her head was swimming with confusion. If that was what had happened, that meant someone had ordered Kyander to set a trap for them. But that surely meant that her father had come across something monstrous, because you didn't kill four people, including a child, for an accounting mistake or a poor recruitment choice. What could that have been, though? Something involving the Nazis, because her father had been revolted at the idea of having to cooperate with them? If what Kyander had said was true, of course. That was the thing with shadows. Depending on how the light fell, the same scary shadow could be thrown by something mammoth, like a government conspiracy, or by something tiny, like a bruised ego. You could never tell.

Hella frowned, trying to remember what she had read about the fate of the Jewish prisoners of war. There had not been many of them, certainly less than a thousand. They had been sent to a labour camp in Lapland and to another one in Suursaari, an island in the Gulf of Finland, where the police thought they could be isolated from the rest of the population. As far as Hella knew, they had not been treated badly and had been released after the war. No one in Finland had suffered the atrocities of the Nazi death camps. No one had died.

She shivered, suddenly cold, even though no wind was blowing off the sea. Her father had never told them what had happened in the Suursaari camp, but he had returned to Helsinki angry and upset. She should have listened more. She should have asked him. At eighteen, she should have known. Too late now.

The seagulls scattered, flapping their wings, as Hella rose from her bench. She still did not see what danger her father could have represented to anybody. It was not like he was planning to write his memoirs, not like Kyander was.

She would never know what happened, that was the worst part. She thought about a dream she had sometimes, a dream where she found the truck driver, took careful aim and pulled the trigger – *bam*. In those dreams, she could never imagine him as an ordinary person: a man buying groceries, say, or helping his child with homework, or reading a novel. In her mind, he was always driving, the wheel held loosely in big hairy hands. But that was not true. He could have been anybody. She doubted Kyander would have done the dirty work himself – he was not the type. And as things stood, she had no proof that he was even involved. All she had was a hunch. Worthless feminine intuition. They'd laugh in her face if she went about accusing him.

The sun's rays were reflecting on the water, blinding her. A young couple passed, holding hands. Behind them, a man was dragging his suitcase over the cobblestones. Hella thought briefly of going back to the station, waiting there until the mysterious, Russian-speaking vagabond showed up, but she'd go mad if she had to wait around for days and days. A better course of action would be to go through the papers her father had left behind in his study at home. Even though Hella didn't hold out much hope – if the murder had been orchestrated by someone at the SUPO, there was no doubt they had made sure that no damning evidence had been left behind – she had to try. She had a dim recollection of the weeks that followed her family's death, although she did remember a visit from Kyander. He had brought her red, scentless carnations, and a shop-wrapped pastry. After patting her awkwardly on the back and offering her his handkerchief, he had told her that he needed to check her father's office, to make sure nothing confidential had been left behind. Hella hadn't objected;

why would she have done? She hadn't even found it strange that he'd spent so much time in there with the door closed, or the fact that he'd finally emerged from it with his leather briefcase bursting at the seams.

If someone, some kindly fairy (that had been notably absent from Hella's life so far) had offered her a choice to get her family back in exchange for a state secret, she would have done it gladly. She'd still do it today, in a heartbeat. But unless your name was Orpheus, you could never bring back the dead. And because kindly fairies didn't exist but state secrets did, Hella was going to do the next best thing. She was going to find out what it was that her father knew and someone at the SUPO wanted him to forget. And then, once she found it, she was going to use that information to avenge their deaths.

32

Hella didn't need to look around her to remember every nook and cranny, every creaking floorboard and faded photograph in her family home. From the dusty metal ashtray on the mantelpiece to the old pair of felt boots in the broom cupboard, from the assorted volumes of the *Kalevala* to a fountain pen on its marble pedestal, she knew it as well as she knew her own face. Better even, because her face had never interested her all that much. Over the past eleven years, the house had stood abandoned and alone, gathering dust. Keeping its secrets. Biding its time.

She ran a hand along the leather-bound volumes lining the walls of her father's study. Atlases. Poetry. Dictionaries. Pinned to the wall opposite the window, a large map of the Soviet Union – one-sixth of the Earth's surface, coloured in an aggressive blood red – and the tiny grey map of Finland next to it. A stack of paper next to the typewriter. Hella held the topmost sheet to the light: there was no imprint on it. Same with the typewriter ribbon. Her brow furrowed, Hella fumbled in her pocket and pulled out a *salmiakki* lozenge. A bit of fluff was stuck to it; she brushed it off and popped the candy into her mouth. Her father's notebooks were all gone, same as the desktop calendar. At the time, Kyander had invoked national security, and she had believed him. But if her father had something to hide, he wouldn't have written it in a notebook or on a calendar anyway. Where, then? Under the floorboards? In her favourite children's book, the one about Baba Yaga and the house on chicken legs? Between the pages of a dictionary? Hella sighed. Kyander must have looked in all those places already, though she would check anyway. If only she knew what she was looking for. A letter, a string of numbers, like the ones her mysterious correspondent had sent her? She decided she would know when she found it. *If* she found it. No, not if. There was bound to be something; she couldn't believe that, whatever it was, Kyander had taken it away. She would not give up until she knew. She was her father's daughter, after all.

Five hours later, Hella stood looking through the window as the light outside slowly waned. She had long since stopped pulling cobwebs out of her hair and wood splinters out of her fingers, and her back ached as if she was a peasant woman who had spent her day in the fields. And still there was nothing. No secret hiding place or messages written in code or unexplained photographs stuck between the pages of some never-read novel. Or, if there were, she hadn't found them.

On the small side table by the window, there was a half-played chess game, left in progress for eleven years. Hella wondered idly if her father had been playing black or white, not that it mattered: either way, he'd been good. But not good enough not to get himself killed.

Hella hadn't realized she was crying until she ran the back of her hand across her face and noticed it was wet. She was getting nowhere, failing at everything. She thought

159

of Veikko Aalto's dead body slumped at the bottom of the stairs, another one that the midsummer night's dew would not heal.

Outside, the street was quiet, not a person in sight, only tree branches swaying in the breeze and a stray cat running along Erkki Kanerva's fence. He had knocked on her door at around six in the evening, but she hadn't felt like seeing him, and so she'd stepped aside into the shadow of the curtains and waited until he was gone. All in all, the day had been too much, and the last thing she wanted was company, having to smile and chat and pretend.

Hella closed her eyes as images from the day returned. Would things have been different if she'd gone to see Heikkinen the night before, as she had initially planned? She would have told him that she suspected Veikko Aalto of murdering Maria, probably out of spite. That she thought she knew what had happened but had no proof. Then what? She had no way of knowing Aalto would choose that night to try to set fire to his cousin's house after all these years. And yet Hella had that ridiculous feeling of responsibility, of not being where she should have been when disaster struck. Above all, she couldn't shake off the feeling of having failed. Or having missed something important, which was just another word for failing.

She picked up the white knight from the chessboard and held it up to the evening light. The figurine was old, carved out of ivory, and warm to her touch. Her father was a white knight, in his own way. She had inherited that absolute intolerance to injustice from him. And what else?

Like most murder victims, Hella's father had died because of who he was. It always came down to that, in the end. The choices people made, and their inevitable consequences. She tried to imagine her father the way other people might have seen him, but the image wouldn't come into focus. A dedicated professional. A patriot. A senior official at the SUPO. All that was true, but to her, he had just been Dad. The man who read her bedtime stories and taught her not to be afraid of the dark. The man who always took the time to listen and consider the implications before offering her his advice. The man who was killed, betrayed by his best friend.

33

Jokela's legs were crossed, one foot jumping like it was about to take off. He had abandoned his desk chair for a Chesterfield sofa wedged between the fireplace and the window, and by his elbow there was a glass in a silver holder. The glass was filled to the brim with an amber liquid that Hella hoped was weak tea.

Jokela patted the sofa next to him. "I thought you'd come yesterday."

Hella shrugged, sitting down. "I'm sure Inspector Pinchus already told you about what happened. I'm only here because you promised to check on my parents' file. Did you ask the officer at the archives what happened to it?"

Jokela didn't seem to have heard her. "Well, I'm glad you're here now. I mean, you know Pinchus." Jokela lifted the glass and Hella saw with relief that a small silver spoon was sticking out of it. Definitely tea. He pulled a lump of sugar from somewhere behind the sofa, dropped it into his drink and stirred. "The problem with Pinchus is that he can't ever say yes or no, it's always *on the one hand* this, *on the other hand* that. Annoying as hell. Every time I have to discuss a case with him, I have to keep reminding myself to breathe slowly, or bring cigarettes, or both. Anyway. He seems to think it was self-defence, with death resulting from a fall down the stairs, but until your pal Räikkönen has absolutely eliminated curare poisoning and the intervention of evil spirits, he won't say anything for sure. He'll just sit there, hunched like a heron, and drone on about being too old for this job – which is also annoying, because he's a good few years younger than me." Jokela took a noisy slurp of his tea and looked at her. "What I don't understand is why the other guy, the weird one, went to Heikkinen's house in the first place. What do you think?"

This was new, Hella thought. Jokela being interested in *why*, as opposed to *who* and *when*. "I don't know," she said slowly. "I think it's possible that Veikko Aalto became fixated on his cousin – that happens frequently in families. Maybe he wanted to punish him for being successful. That was why he sent those letters here and —"

Jokela waved an impatient hand. "And so he decided to go over there in the dead of night, with a canister full of petrol? You think he killed the wife, too? Same – what do they call it? – *modus operandi*? Fire in the night and, *boom*, gone?"

"I believe that is indeed what happened to Mrs Heikkinen," Hella said carefully. "The difference is, Mr Heikkinen woke up and could defend himself."

"Not very well, though." Jokela gave her a puzzled frown. "I mean he was what, three feet away, and he shot and missed? Good thing we weren't planning on employing him as an ordinary policeman. Still, I suppose knowing how to shoot isn't a prerequisite to being a good head of department."

"So you're still planning on appointing him?"

"Not immediately." Jokela shook his head. "Wouldn't do, we need to let the dust settle a bit. Besides —"

Hella cut him off. "Of course. I understand. Look, about my parents' file. I don't suppose the SUPO could have removed the contents, could they?"

"Actually, I wouldn't put it past them." Jokela struck a match and lit a cigarette. "They have this bad habit of thinking that nothing is out of bounds." He screwed his mouth to one side to blow smoke away from her face. "You still want to investigate, then?"

"Why, would you recommend I don't do that? Let sleeping dogs lie? Jon, this is my family we're talking about." She heard her voice rise, saw Jokela squirm, but continued nonetheless. "I know nothing will bring them back. I still want to know what happened."

There was a silence. Jokela puffed his cheeks before letting out a long, slow breath. "It was me who took the file. When you told me you wanted to see it, I knew it was a bad idea. So I got to the office early the following day, and I asked the officer on duty to bring it to me, and I took out the contents."

Hella stared at him, appalled. "But why?"

"Because I wanted to protect you; is that so hard to understand? A young girl" – he threw an appraising glance at her – "well, maybe not *young*, but still. I don't want anything bad to happen to you. Can't you understand that?"

So she was right, Hella thought. It was some sort of state secret. Something dangerous, anyway. And no one would tell her. She rose. "I wish you'd stop being so good to me. It's insulting, because it somehow implies that I'm part of some group who cannot think for themselves: children, imbeciles, women. And, as you said, I'm not that young. So how about I make up my own mind?" She turned and headed for the door, swallowing down the insults that rose like bile in her throat. Where could she find help now? Maybe Heikkinen —

"There was another one, you know," Jokela said to her retreating back.

I don't care, Hella wanted to scream. "I never want to see you again. Ever."

"Even though Aalto's dead," Jokela said.

Hella yanked the door handle. Then whipped around. "What?"

"Like I told you. There was another letter. Anonymous." Jokela crushed his cigarette in the overflowing ashtray. "Text's the same. It was posted yesterday afternoon, so it couldn't have been Aalto." Jokela's small eyes were boring into her. "But like you said, I'm the bad guy and you never want to set foot in this office again."

Hella thought about it. She was free to go, of course. And she'd meant what she said about Jokela. But another anonymous letter… It changed everything. This case was about to blow up in their faces. The same word that came into her mind when she'd first heard about the dead dog started reverberating, spinning out of control. Trouble. This case was trouble. She had tried to put a lid on her instincts about it, but she couldn't.

Hella closed the door softly and turned to face Jokela.

"Let me see it."

34

Hella could still hear her father's voice, slightly hoarse from too much smoking, but patient and kind, asking her: "What do you see?"

The picture was black and white, just silhouettes really. "Two faces," she replied. "A man and a woman, though they do look alike, and they're leaning towards each other. As if they're whispering something, or are about to kiss."

Her father moved the picture a little, placing it under the circle of yellow light thrown by the table lamp. They were in the living room, curtains drawn against the dark February night – a short time, Hella realized now, before the fatal hit-and-run.

"You don't see a vase?" her father asked.

"What vase? No…" She picked up the picture and moved it closer to her face. "I only see faces."

Her father chuckled. "Focus on the white now. The space between the faces."

"Oh…" Hella drew a sharp breath. Now she had seen the vase, the two lovers had melted into the background, as if they hadn't existed at all. "It *is* a vase. How strange."

"It's an optical illusion, created by a man called Edgar Rubin in 1915. The drawing is ambiguous, it plays with our perception. Some people even say it's a showcase of unintentional blindness. Your brain fixates on one thing and is unable to see the other image."

"But if I want to join the police," Hella said, "I'd need to be able to see both."

Her father winked. "I can imagine you becoming the first woman ever on the homicide squad. And if one day you're stuck on a difficult case, just think of Rubin's vase."

Hella blinked and Senate Square's neoclassical splendour came back into focus: a seagull perched on top of the bronze statue of Tsar Alexander II, the green domes of the cathedral against the azure blue of the sky, the white columns of the university. The anonymous letter that Jokela had given her was in her handbag, and it did not require an expert in graphology to know that it had been written in the same hand. And the postmark was sharp, no smudges or doubts as to the date – as Jokela had told her, the letter had been posted the previous afternoon, when Veikko Aalto was already lying on a slab in Tom's morgue, ready to be dissected.

But if the letters had not been written by Heikkinen's mad cousin, if someone else was stalking Heikkinen, that changed everything. Hella frowned, thinking back to the previous morning. In her mind's eye, she could see the living room clearly, as if the image of the deep, comfortable sofas and the tall windows framed by silk curtains, the graceful sideboards and the curving oak staircase were directly imprinted on her retinas. So Heikkinen had surprised someone he thought was a burglar. It happened at that hour when sleep is at its heaviest, and there was the element of surprise, too. Hella supposed it was possible he hadn't recognized his cousin, even at close range. That wasn't what was bothering her, though. Or not only that.

Why had Aalto come? When prodded, Heikkinen could offer no explanation. A simple coincidence? That sort of thing could happen. Still, that was another thing to add to her growing list of questions.

Hella pulled the anonymous letter out of her handbag and smoothed it on her lap, squinting because the sunlight moved fitfully across the square and glittered on the roofs and windows. So, she had one dead dog, one sleeping pill overdose, one house fire. A murdered woman and her inconsolable widower, who had nearly perished attempting to save her. She also had Tom and the SUPO, who had both looked into it, and had both concluded accident or suicide. As for the fire, no one seemed to know. There was nothing about it in Tom's file. Had it started on its own, or had someone – Heikkinen's mad cousin? – come over with a can full of petrol? He'd been there, after all, the last person to see Maria alive. As for the dog… The dog – and this was important – had died before the woman had. And Aalto was mad, everyone agreed on that, just like everyone agreed that he hated his cousin. It all made sense. And at the same time… Was there a different way to look at it, could she tilt the picture to the light again and see a vase instead of the two faces? And were the means and opportunity everything? Because there was one question that she had forgotten to ask herself: who could have wanted Maria dead? And why? Or – going back to the beginning – could it have been a suicide after all?

Hella looked up, at the white cumulus clouds now running across the blue expanse of sky, and then down, at a sparrow hopping at her feet in search of crumbs. One of the bird's wings was drooping, seemingly broken. She opened her handbag, but she had no bread and no cookies to offer to the tiny creature, and the sparrow, scared by the metallic snap of the clasp, hopped away awkwardly. The air was warm and sweet and still, and the sun was hot on Hella's forearms. On a day like this, it was difficult to believe that evil could be lurking behind the glistening paintwork and the elegant sloped roofs, that it could find a place to hide in the brightest of sunlit rooms. But for all her desire to believe in humanity's general order and kindness, there was no denying that sometimes the tiniest shift of perspective made you see everything anew. She thought of Tom, who was doing the autopsy on Veikko Aalto, and how she had seen him two days earlier and he had told her about the inventors of the heart-lung machine. She thought of the photograph she had seen in Aalto's house, cockroaches running along the frame, and of the one that took pride of place on Heikkinen's marble mantelpiece. It was the same woman, she realized with a jolt. It was just her smile that was different.

Above all, though, Hella thought of Rubin's vase. Of the shadow and light, of things as they are and things as they seem to be. Her heart sank. What she was looking at was a perfect crime.

And she had no chance in hell of proving that it had happened.

She stared down at the letter. She now had a good idea as to who its author might be, but there was only one way to know for sure. Hella put the letter carefully back into her handbag and rose from the bench.

35

"Does it ever cross your mind," Tom said, "that I might *just* happen to be busy at the time you decide you need to see me immediately?"

"Were you?" Hella glanced at the samovar on the counter, boiling water gushing from its tap, and at the mean-looking server who was filling their tea glasses.

Tom shook his head regretfully. "As it happens, no. But I could have been. An autopsy…"

"That's exactly why I wanted to see you." She smiled at Tom, but he didn't smile back.

The cafe was anything but welcoming. A tiny place, just five roughly cut pine tables, sombre and over-furnished. It looked like nothing had changed here since the days old Russian immigrants drank scalding hot tea from the samovar and vodka from narrow glasses. They were not at home here; Hella had sensed that as soon as they had crossed the threshold, but by then, it was too late.

The server placed two glasses of tea ensconced in tarnished silver holders in front of them and withdrew sullenly. Tom rolled his eyes, reaching for the sugar bowl in front of him. It was empty. He sighed. "So, what's the story? Do you want to know if I found anything unusual during Aalto's autopsy?"

Hella raised an eyebrow. "Did you?"

"No. Way too undernourished, but otherwise he was in good health." Tom shifted in his seat. The great bulk of him barely fit behind the small table. "That is, until he fell down the stairs and broke his neck."

"No proof that Heikkinen pushed him?"

"None at all. As far as I'm concerned, it all happened exactly as Heikkinen described it. Why are you asking?"

"I just thought..." Hella lowered her voice. The server was lurking by the samovar, trying to look uninterested, but she could see him throwing glances at them when he thought no one would notice. "I just thought, what if it all happened the other way around? Actually, you're the one who put the idea in my head."

"I did?" Tom grimaced as he took another sip of his tea. "Do you think they brew this with coal tar?"

"It was when you told me that story about whatshisname who invented the heart-lung machine."

"John Gibbon."

"That guy. You said that he and his wife had lured stray cats from the street, to try and see if their machine worked."

"Yes. So?"

"Remember I told you about Veikko Aalto killing his neighbour's dog? It happened a few days before Maria died. I always thought he was testing out the drug, making sure it worked, but what if it was the other way around? What if he found out that her husband had been giving her the drug, and he wanted to check if it was dangerous?"

"Huh," Tom said. "Possible."

"And there's something else. The neighbour, Mr Sopanen, also said that Aalto had been OK then. I didn't pick up on it at the time, but doesn't that suggest he became the way he was – malnourished, crazy – *after* Maria died?"

171

"You think he went mad because he was devastated? That he was in love with her?"

Hella shrugged. "Heikkinen told me himself that they had been close. Maria's mother said it too."

Tom swilled the tea in his cup, frowning. "I don't know," he said finally. "Could be, of course, but it could also play the other way. Depends how you look at it."

"Exactly!" Hella's voice must have been too loud, because the server dropped the stained cloth he was using to polish the counter. "That's *exactly* it. A perfect crime." She sighed. "And I can't prove it."

Tom pulled his wallet out of his pocket and gestured to the server. "What about the anonymous letters? Do you know who wrote them?"

"That's not a great mystery, I'm afraid. Just one more thing I should have seen earlier and didn't. But my mother died when I was still young, so I never realized I was supposed to inherit the family recipes. Shall we go? I don't want to keep you away from your work."

36

"So you liked the pancake then, did you? I thought you did. Well, no wonder, it's an old family recipe. A success every time I make it, you can't go wrong with it. Do you want the recipe for the steamed prunes as well?"

Hella smiled. "Yes please." She was once again sitting in Liisa Vanhanen's living room, a cup of coffee on the table before her, while her hostess copied down the recipe. "I enjoyed it very much," she added primly. "As much as your mother's *vorschmack* recipe." Which she had seen at the Vanhanens' summer cabin and which of course had been written down in the older woman's hand. Now, glancing over at Mrs Vanhanen's small, upright handwriting, Hella thought that she'd been stupid not to realize it earlier. As she had expected, Maria's sister was the one who had written the letters, and the recipe she was copying proved it. Although an expert in graphology would be able to confirm it, there was no need. Most anonymous letter writers change the slant and the size of the characters, trying to hide their identity. The prudent ones push further by changing the loops on the *y*'s, the capital *A*'s and the crossbars on the *t*'s, but Hella had yet to see one who remembered to vary the intervals at which they lifted pen from paper – and here she could see it was every three letters, like in the blackmail letter she had in her handbag.

Hella took a bite out of her *pulla* and chewed it meditatively, considering the implications. For some reason, Liisa Vanhanen hated her brother-in-law to the point of going to all that trouble, and yet, when Hella had showed up on her doorstep and asked in confidence for her thoughts on Johannes Heikkinen, she'd had nothing but praise for him. Why?

"I bet you grew up without a mother," Liisa said, folding the recipe in two and pushing it towards Hella.

"My parents died in a traffic accident when I was eighteen." Hella slipped the recipe into her handbag. "Thank you very much. If I follow it step by step, do you think I'll succeed?"

Liisa Vanhanen looked at her with an expression that was trying hard not to be condescending. "If you follow all the steps, very carefully and in order, then yes."

"Thank you," Hella said, again. Then she added: "I lied to you about working at the SUPO. I'm sorry about that."

There was a silence, only troubled by the loud ticking of a grandfather clock. Hella forced herself to meet her hostess's gaze. The woman was staring at her, eyebrows raised. Her voice, when it finally came, was high-pitched and incredulous. "And why did you do that?"

"I needed a pretext to talk to you, and it was as good a story as any." Hella shrugged. "At least, that's what I believed at the time, but I was obviously wrong. You might have trusted me if I'd told you the truth."

The woman was still looking at her, as if trying to make up her mind. "And I believed you!" The poodle curls shook in despair – or outrage; Hella wasn't sure.

She answered the unspoken question. "I'm a private

investigator, working with the police. They have received your letters."

"I didn't send any letters to the police." But now Liisa Vanhanen was avoiding her gaze.

Hella opened her handbag. "I have one with me. We can compare it with the recipe you just wrote down. I could show you the similarities, but I trust that won't be necessary." She smiled with more confidence than she felt. If Liisa Vanhanen thought about it at all, she'd realize soon enough that Hella had not entered her home in any official capacity, and that she could throw her out any time she liked and refuse to answer her questions. Hella's only advantage was knowing this, and making sure the other woman didn't have enough time to think. "It's all right, no one's going to prosecute you for the letters. But I need to know why you wrote them. And why you lied to me."

She knew why, of course, or she thought she knew. But knowing was one thing, and proving it a completely different matter. She thought about the yellow living room at Heikkinen's house, the deep plush carpets and draperies over the narrow barred windows. Of the house's thick, soundproofed walls and of the piano playing late into the night. Liisa Vanhanen remained silent, hands clasped in her lap, the wedding ring of dull gold biting into the flesh of her finger. Hella said: "Your mother implied that Maria was a bit of an attention-seeker. Would you agree with that assessment?"

A slow shake of the head. "No."

"Then what was she like?"

"Naive. Or maybe *stupid* would be a better word. She had a husband who loved her."

Hella remembered the photograph she had seen when she first went to visit Heikkinen, of a pale sickly creature

175

in a knitted shawl. A mouse of a woman. But apparently a spirited mouse. "She had a husband who loved her, but she didn't love him back. Is that what happened?"

Liisa Vanhanen rose and walked over to the window, through which Hella could see the straggling hedge which bordered the garden. "Mother always said we should be content with what we have. My husband isn't Prince Charming, but then, I'm not a fairy-tale princess either, and we're fine, we really are. But Maria... Everything that happened, it was her fault."

"Because love is the most dangerous thing," Hella said. "More dangerous even than hate. That, and the desire to control."

"I never understood what she saw in Veikko. It's true that he was good-looking once, but in a brooding sort of way, and he had no prospects in life. Not marriage material, not by a long shot. Mother had been hoping she'd forget him, in time, especially given that he went away for a few months, to write his sonnets in Paris or whatever it is that poets do. And when Johannes proposed to Maria, everyone was overjoyed."

"Your sister too?"

A bitter laugh. "No, not her, you couldn't say that. Though in the end she agreed to marry him. Mother insisted so much, and so did I. They were married the following month."

"And how did it go?"

The woman turned to look at her, but it was impossible to gauge the expression in those blue, unblinking eyes. If her voice held any emotion, it was resignation. "How do you think? I suppose, at first, everyone thought they'd be all right. Johannes kept bringing her flowers, and he bought that big, beautiful apartment, and Maria seemed content with that. And Veikko was still in Europe, doing God knows what, so we thought she had forgotten all about him, moved on. And then Maria fell pregnant, and she was so happy, like she was walking on air…"

Suddenly, Hella noticed that the woman was crying. Her face didn't change, but now tears were streaming down her cheeks, bright as pearls. Hella said, gently, "And then the baby died."

"Yes. And Maria… She just spiralled out of control. She turned into a shadow, her face grey and absent. And she lost so much weight she looked like she was made of sticks. She never cried, but she didn't speak much either, and she kept bumping into things, falling over and losing her balance. Or at least that's what she told me when I asked her about the cuts and bruises." Liisa Vanhanen was tripping over her words now in her haste to explain. "We were all worried sick about her. You got this feeling that Maria had something fundamental broken inside her, and the best she could do was to take a polite interest in things, but not for too long."

"Was Veikko Aalto back in Helsinki by that time?" Hella asked.

"Yes." The woman hesitated. "They saw each other a lot. As friends." There was a hint of defensiveness in her voice, as if the thought that her long-dead sister could have been unfaithful to her husband was intolerable.

Hella nodded. "And that was when Johannes Heikkinen made the decision to kill his wife."

37

It seemed to Hella that the room had grown darker, that the sun had slid behind the clouds, but maybe it was an illusion. For a long time, neither of them spoke. Then Liisa Vanhanen said dully, "There's no proof."

"None at all," Hella confirmed. "Just like there's no proof that your sister's cuts and bruises were the result of domestic abuse, not her being clumsy." Hella looked down at her hands, still clutching the handbag. She set it down. "Heikkinen is a very good liar, maybe because he's so utterly and sincerely convinced that he's one of the good guys, the best there is. The rest flows from there, and he can explain away just about anything. He probably thinks that not only did his wife get what she deserved, it was the right thing to do. Otherwise, he wouldn't have done it. Oh yes, he's an exceptional liar." Hella looked at the woman attentively. "Which is why I'm surprised you suspected him. Did Maria confide in you before her death?"

"They both did." Liisa Vanhanen swallowed hard, as if there was something ragged and sharp stuck in her throat. "Maria and Veikko. But I didn't believe them."

Hella's voice remained carefully sympathetic. "What did they tell you?"

"Veikko, he…" Liisa Vanhanen shook her head. "He was incoherent. It took me a while to understand what he was saying. What it boiled down to, in the end, was that Maria was being poisoned by her husband." She glanced at Hella. "But it seemed so absurd! And every time I saw Johannes, he was always so sweet and nice to Maria, a perfect gentleman. I told Veikko that he was surely mistaken, but he kept repeating these bizarre claims in a panicked voice. He wouldn't tell me what evidence he had, or why he would think that." Liisa Vanhanen dragged a hand across her eyes to wipe away tears. "And he was so vague on details, and angry that I found his story unbelievable. In the end, he asked me to go to the police with him. And when I refused, he became angrier still, told me I was 'one of them', whatever that meant. So no, I didn't believe him."

"And Maria?"

"Maria was the opposite. She barely said a thing. Just that she'd had a lot of trouble sleeping lately, and the medicine her doctor gave her wasn't helping, so Johannes had found a new drug for her, and she was sleeping so much better. She smiled when she said that, a sad little smile, but a smile nonetheless. And then she said that it was a good thing. That Johannes had been upset with her lately, and her finally sleeping well at night calmed him down." Liisa Vanhanen drew a shaky breath. "And then the next week there was the fire, and she was dead. And it was too late."

Hella looked at the woman, who was sitting with her head turned away, her thin hands alternatively smoothing and plucking at her apron. So Liisa Vanhanen had known what had happened, but she didn't have any proof. Still, if Hella was in her place, she would have —

"You never thought of going to the police?"

The woman paused for a few seconds before replying, as if marshalling her thoughts. "I thought about it, but I wasn't sure. I knew Johannes had tried to save Maria, that he'd been hurt doing so. So I talked to my mother. I was afraid to tell her I suspected Johannes, so I started by saying that I'd noticed how unhappy Maria had been lately. And you know what she said? 'So, my daughter has a broken heart. Big deal! I broke my arm once and I suffered terribly, but I didn't make a fuss over it!' After that, of course, I said nothing. And then, when I went to see Veikko, he refused to talk to me. He was overcome with grief, and I think he was angry at me for letting Maria down, but I still thought we could go to the police together..."

"Veikko was probably afraid," Hella said. "You see, he had tried to assess how dangerous the drug was, and he gave some to his neighbours' dog and it died. Johannes must have found out about it, I don't know how. Maybe Veikko told him himself. And so Johannes told his cousin that no one would believe him, that everyone would think *he* was the murderer."

Hella thought of the pathetic figure she had encountered in Puu-Vallila, about Veikko Aalto's shaky hands, dirty clothes and incoherent speech. If the man had been unable to convince Liisa, what chance had he of convincing a homicide squad inspector? And you'd need nerve *and* irrefutable proof to go about accusing an upstanding SUPO official of domestic abuse and murder.

"I actually think that was Johannes' plan. He would give himself a good role to play trying to save Maria and accusing his cousin of killing her. But he hadn't expected to get hurt in the fire, and when he finally came to, the pathologist and the SUPO had both concluded that Maria's death had been an accident, and it was too late for him to do anything without drawing attention to himself." Hella smiled bitterly. "That was why he was so excited when I came along, asking him about his cousin and his wife's death. He thought it was his chance to reopen the investigation, that I would act in his interest. And I believed him."

"Everyone always believes him." Liisa Vanhanen's face looked older now, dragged down around the edges. "And he'll still go unpunished, and now Veikko is dead and my letters haven't achieved anything."

"I'll talk to the police," Hella said. "I'll talk to the pathologist, too. He noted in his report that there were bruises on Maria's body. At the very least, we'll stop him from getting this job."

"Do you really believe that?"

"I do," Hella said. "Absolutely." That wasn't true, but she couldn't bring herself to admit it. She was still hoping she'd find a way to make Johannes Heikkinen pay for his crimes. She thought about it all the way back to her house, coming up with ideas before discarding them, hoping against hope that someone – Jokela, Heikkinen's SUPO superiors, the press – would listen to her. When she finally turned into her street, she was still thinking about what she should do. That's when she saw a tall, stooping figure in a grey overcoat on her doorstep and forgot to think, or to breathe.

38

For a moment, Hella couldn't move. She just stood there, gasping for air, her eyes fixed on the tall grey figure now cupping his hands against her window and peering inside. In the blinding sun, with his out-of-season coat hanging in long creases from his narrow shoulders, he looked more like a scarecrow than a real person. Hella blinked. Should she call out to him? Or approach him carefully, slowly, so as not to scare the man away? What did he want from her? There was a bulging backpack at his feet, as grey and scuffed as the rest of his person. Hella inched closer, her feet heavy as lead, her head swimming. Then, slowly, perhaps feeling her gaze on the back of his neck, the man uncupped his hands from the window and turned to face her. His eyes were sunk deep in his head, and she thought she saw a tattoo in blue ink on his left forearm. Hella quickened her step, then, seeing the man grab his backpack, broke into a run. "Wait," she cried. "Please!" How did you say it in Russian? "*Podozhdite! Pozhaluista!*"

He was sprinting down the street now, awkwardly, his sticklike legs dragged down by his huge black boots, the long coat flowing behind him like a cape or a sail. The man's legs were much longer than Hella's, but he was no match for her fury and determination. She was already closing in on him, the dark coat within her grasp, when her heel broke with a snap, her right foot caught on the pavement and she fell forward, landing on all fours. "Wait!"

The man didn't stop, didn't even pause to look back. He kept running, as fast as he could, and when Hella finally managed to pull herself back onto her feet, he was already turning the corner. It was too late. She was too late. Still, she kicked off her useless shoes and ran, her heart jammed in her throat, but when she turned the corner, the street was empty. Just a stray cat strolling nonchalantly across the road. Hella glanced at the windows of the houses on either side, hoping to spot a housewife peering through her net curtains, someone who might have told her where the man had gone, but the windows were as empty as the street. She turned back, cursing under her breath. Both her knees were scraped, and when she opened her hand-bag to take out her keys, she saw that her right hand was blue and swollen.

Once inside the house, Hella slumped on the sofa, feeling angry and miserable, wondering if the man in the grey coat would ever show up again. Why had he run if he kept coming back, if he'd written her a note asking her to meet him at Central Station? It didn't make sense. She knew that she needed to go to the bathroom, to wash the dirt and the blood off her knees. She also needed a drink, and then she needed to change her clothes and find some ice for her hand. Hella held it up to the light for inspection. It was just a bruise, but a large one; she had trouble closing her fist. Oh damn. Ever since she had moved back into her childhood home, things had been going from bad to worse. Maybe she should put the house on the market and move to Lapland. Although they wouldn't want her back at the police station, presumably she was capable of finding another job.

With her left hand, she could just about reach the pine chest in which her mother stored her linen and fancy dinner plates and her father kept the alcohol they served at dinner parties. The bottle of vodka was grey with dust, but the smell and taste had not been altered by the years. Her throat burned when she took a swig. Then she pulled a handkerchief out of her handbag, soaked it with vodka and pressed it to her knee. She was still thinking about the man. What if it hadn't been her he wanted to see? What if he'd been hoping to see her father, because somehow he didn't know that Colonel Mauzer was dead? Suddenly, Hella thought of something. The letters left by the scarecrow in grey were still on the coffee table. She picked them up. The latest one was on top, and Hella squinted at it, wondering how she could have missed it. The letter had been addressed to *H.M.* That meant Hella Mauzer, she had assumed at the time. But it was written in Russian, and she had not spoken that language for a long time and had forgotten how tricky it was. In Russian, the letter that looks like a capital *H* is really an *N*. As in Niklas Mauzer.

Hella blew out a long, disconcerted breath, marvelling at her own stupidity. That letter, and all the previous ones, had been meant for her father. That was why her visitor had run when he saw her, that was why he hadn't approached her as she stood waiting at the railway station. He didn't want to see her, he only wanted Colonel Mauzer. Which meant the man didn't know that her father had been dead for over a decade, probably because he'd been away all those years and had only just arrived in Helsinki. He was also a Soviet. Hella thought about the newspaper headlines she had seen recently, of the faces of prisoners newly released from Gulag camps. The man in grey had the same sort of face, creased and colourless, the result of persistent starvation and inhumane treatment, of smoke-filled barracks and freezing Arctic wind against the skin. He also seemed to have very poor eyesight, and he probably didn't speak much Finnish. That could go some way towards explaining why he believed her father was still alive; he might have glimpsed Steve's silhouette behind the curtains and thought it was him. But why had he come? Had he been in Finland before? What in his past had he wanted to come to terms with, or maybe set right, that had compelled him to undertake that perilous journey from the Soviet Union all the way to Hella's little house by the sea? That man was someone her father had once known, she was sure of it. Maybe someone he had met during his work with the prisoners of war? What had Kyander said, that her father had been charged with watching over the Russian Jews? And that he wasn't really cooperative, where Nazis were involved?

And suddenly she knew. The certainty did not come like a bolt of lightning, or present itself in the form of a puzzle's missing piece, clicking satisfyingly into place. It came as a kick to the stomach, and she nearly doubled over, her body ringing with pain but her mind clear for the first time in a long while. For a moment she sat absolutely still, her gaze lost in a distant landscape that had seen so many men march to their deaths. If she was right, here was the secret worth killing for. And not only one man; a whole family. She didn't need to look at the numbers, she knew them by heart: *169062*. Not someone's telephone number. Not a lock combination, or a message written in code. She thought of the man she'd just seen, of the blue tattoo on his left forearm. She probably would have guessed earlier if she'd ever heard of anyone from Finland having been deported to Auschwitz. It was the only camp that had tattooed its inmates.

Hella rose with difficulty and made her way on shaky legs to her father's study. The map was still tacked to the wall, and she ran a finger along the lines until she found the island that the Finnish called Suursaari and the Soviets Hogland. So this was where those poor men, women and children had lived, fearing for their lives while the war raged all around them. Most of them had come back from the island. Most, but not all. Her mysterious visitor must have been shipped to Auschwitz. Her father had certainly opposed that plan, and he had paid the price. But what had the Nazis promised to Kyander? What promotion or money or privilege would make him send innocent men to a death camp? Or had he done it of his own accord because he was so afraid of the communists that he was eager and willing to make a pact with the devil? She closed her eyes. Like everyone else, she had seen the photographs of the death camps, and she had heard the stories. The gas chambers, the mutilations and the executions, children separated from their mothers, men made to dig their own graves. But this one man had lived through hell and managed to come back. And he was key to solving her family's murder.

39

"How do I find a Soviet who's here illegally?"

"How do you find a needle in a haystack?"

Steve laughed, but Hella didn't echo him. She had barged into his house as soon as he opened the door, pushing past a clothes rack overburdened with parkas and into the living room, which was a mess just like her own. Now she was standing watching him with disapproval, hands on hips. "Come on, you're always telling me how you dream of becoming an investigative journalist. I expect you know people."

"Me?" Steve ran a hand through his hair, glancing at her with suspicion. "But why? Is this in connection with your investigation for Jokela?"

"It's in connection with my family's death," Hella said curtly. "And I know almost all of Helsinki's informers and crooks, but I don't know anyone who helps illegal immigrants."

"Would you mind telling me a bit more about why you want to find him?"

Hella shook her head.

"Oh. I see. Well, in that case..." Steve paused, thinking. "I might know people. People who know other people." He motioned towards the sofa. "Why don't you wait here?"

"No. I'm coming with you."

He opened his mouth, probably to tell Hella it wasn't a good idea, but closed it again after one glance at her.

She smiled triumphantly. "Those people who know people – are they in Helsinki?"

"Yes."

She pulled at the sleeves of her cardigan, trying to hide her swollen, bruised hand. "Then let's go."

It turned out to be a long, long day. They went to Ruoholahti first, stopping at a street not far from the Nokia cable factory. Hella waited on the pavement while Steve disappeared inside an ugly apartment building for what seemed like an eternity. The air smelled of lilac and honeysuckle, and a muted song was drifting from somewhere up in the building: *Oy, to ne vecher, to ne vecher...* The singer sounded young, almost a child. *Mne malym malo spalos...* Hella stared at the grimy wall before her, at the broken windows and shrapnel scars and a single pink geranium plant in a clay pot by the door.

When Steve came out, his face was grim. "I didn't know anyone could live with so little." He shook his head, as if trying to dispel the memory. "Anyway, they told me to try a place in the West Harbour. A houseboat. Some Russians have been living there. Some Ukrainians, too. Are you sure your guy's Russian?"

Hella stuck her hands into her cardigan pockets. "A Russian Jew. No doubt about that. No doubt at all."

"OK then." Steve shrugged. "Let's go and find that boat. He must be there."

But the houseboat proved a disappointment. This time, Hella insisted on following Steve onto the slippery deck. Washing had been hung up to dry on a string tied between the masts. No grey coat there. They were all children's clothes: a check pinafore dress, a pair of pink pyjamas. The child herself was inside the cramped, smoke-filled cabin, where the only light came from a tiny window covered with grime. A small pink-clad figure, she was sitting perfectly still on a sofa bed while a woman with a face dragged down by fatigue braided her long blonde hair. She too denied knowing the man that Steve described to her in his hesitant Russian. "Never see him before," the woman said firmly.

"But —" the child said. And then she whimpered as the woman tugged at her hair.

"Never see him before," the woman repeated. She was not looking at them but at some point past them, maybe at the cheap print of a Torah scroll tacked to the wall. It was the only embellishment in a room that otherwise looked as welcoming as a prison cell. No tablecloth, no curtains, no rug, Hella noted. No toys either. What did this child do all day?

Steve made excuses and turned to leave, but Hella was not done there yet. She said, slowly and carefully, with her eyes on the child: "If you ever see him, tell him I wish him no evil. Tell him too that Colonel Mauzer died a long time ago. But I'm his daughter, and I can help. Your man – the man in the grey coat, the man you claim you've never seen in your life – he knows where to find me."

The woman bit her lip and bent lower, her gaze on the child's golden braid. Hella waited for a nod or a word, for any sign of recognition showing that the woman had understood, but there was none. In the end, Hella turned and left. She felt utterly discouraged, because this was the last place to look, and she was sure that they knew something, that they knew that man. They just weren't telling her.

She and Steve decided to walk back to her place. A breeze was blowing off the sea, and the air was cool. Hella pulled her cardigan tighter around herself, sighing. "If only I'd paid more attention to my Russian homework. I would have found the words to convince them."

"Maybe," Steve said. They were heading up Mecheleninkatu. Even though the sun made it look like it was barely afternoon, you could tell it was evening because there were almost no people on the street. Hella was walking with her head down, exhausted after this day full of disappointment.

"Not maybe," she said angrily. "Certainly."

"No. Maybe you found the words, even if your accent is terrible. Look."

She looked. Standing before the low stone wall which marked the outer limit of the green expanse of the Orthodox Cemetery was the child with the golden braid. Right next to her was the man in the grey coat. He was peering myopically at Hella, a confused expression on his face.

Hella stopped, her heart beating fast. The child was speaking to the man in Russian, her eager little face raised up to him. "*Vot eta zhenschina,*" Hella could make out. *This is that woman...* And also: *Mother says could help.* And also: *Dead.* The child was talking about her father now, Hella guessed.

As the man stood still, watching her but not meeting her eye, Hella hesitated. Should she come over to him, introduce herself in her broken Russian? What if he ran again? She decided she'd let him take the initiative, but just then Steve took a big step forward, stuck out his hand and flashed his toothy American grin. "*Dobryi vecher,* I am Steven. Hella's friend."

The man wavered, and Hella cursed under her breath. But the child was keeping a firm grip on his sleeve, determined not to let him escape. After several interminable seconds, the man gave a tiny nod.

"I tell you," he said. "But then I go."

40

To speak to each other, they had to rely on Hella's laborious schoolgirl Russian, complemented by some snippets of peasant Finnish that the man in a grey coat supplied every now and then. *Otkuda. Pochemu. Etsiä. Sota.*

Steve's offer of help had been firmly declined; he now waited between the gravestones, out of earshot, with the child by his side. They made for a curious pair, Hella thought, but so did she and the man in the grey coat. They had stopped by a black marble gravestone bearing the name of Agathon Fabergé, who, Hella thought distractedly, must have been a scion of the famous Russian dynasty of jewellers.

The man in the grey coat was called Yakov and he had lived through hell. He had survived deportation to Auschwitz-Birkenau. Then the Soviet Gulag. He was in Finland illegally, but he had friends – saying that, he glanced at the child, who smiled back and waved – and they were trying to help. He'd thought the colonel could help, too. Given what he knew. That's why he'd come to her house. Was the colonel really dead?

Hella nodded. He really was.

"Killing?" the man asked, matter-of-fact.

"Yes."

There was a silence. Then Yakov sighed. "He a good man."

Hella shivered. "What happened to you? *Chto sluchilos*?"

He hesitated. "It was war. I Jewish, but also Soviet. I surrender. I think safe in Finland. They send me Suursaari, secret island, nobody knows. Almost nobody. One day, they say you, you and you. Come with us. We go Helsinki." There was a long pause, but just as Hella thought he wouldn't say anything else, he went on. "In Helsinki, there's a man. A fat man. Secret Police. He says we must go Estonia, with Gestapo. This man Gestapo friend."

So Yakov had been one of the Jewish prisoners on Suursaari.

"How did my father know? Did you tell him about what happened?"

"I do." He shrugged. "He come to Suursaari before I go, try to help. Give me his name, address. He a good man. Honest. Dead now." He sighed again, then fell silent.

"And then?" Hella said.

"*Potom*?" Yakov glanced down at her, but she wondered if he was really seeing her. It was as if he was looking back at his own past, at the place where he had gone after Suursaari. The skin on his face was mottled and covered in fine lines. A tremor was agitating his right lid. She wondered how old he was. He could have been thirty, or sixty, there was no telling. "*Potom* they take me to Berlin. *Potom Auschwitz*."

"And then?" She could hardly speak.

"I survive. I survive camp, and then they liberate me and make me go Gulag, I survive that too. Now I here." Yakov shivered.

"And the man?" Hella asked. "The fat man. Do you know his name?" She held her breath.

"*Da.* I always remember. Gestapo officer was his friend. The name is Kee-yander."

Of course.

She looked at Yakov. How could she help him, aside from doing the obvious? She'd give him all the money she had, but was there more she could do? Hella no longer had the connections that could offer him a new passport, a new start in life. He needed to speak publicly about what had happened.

"Do you have any proof that you were at Suursaari?" she asked. "I believe you, of course, but for other people to believe you too, we need to" – what was the word – "*dokazatelstvo?*"

He took a step back. "*Nyet.* No *dokazatelstvo,* and no talk again. I go. I live quiet. You no see me. I want forget." He motioned to the child. "*Marina, idyom.*"

"Wait," Hella said. "Please." She fumbled in her handbag, pulling out what markka she had. "Here. Take it."

"No."

In the end, it was the child who took the money. She slid it into her pocket and nodded energetically, her braid swinging. "*Spasibo. Do svidaniya.*"

Hella half-expected her to curtsy. As if it was a social call.

"Wait," Hella said, again. It was all going too fast. "Can we —"

But the child, Marina, cut her off. "No. He doesn't want to see you again. Never. He said so. I heard."

She turned and gripped Yakov by the sleeve, leading him towards the exit. Her pink dress and golden hair made her look like a small but determined fairy leading Yakov out of the valley of death, offering him a second chance at life.

Before Hella could decide what to do next, they were gone.

41

Fear is the most difficult of all emotions to hide because you can literally smell it on a person. No amount of cologne, or coffee, or cardamom can mask its sharp animal tang, that rancid stench that signals prey to its predator. Hella watched as Kyander pulled a check handkerchief out of his pocket and wiped beads of perspiration off his brow.

"It all happened a very long time ago," he said. "I don't really remember."

"Think again," Hella said. She had arrived at Kyander's house as the maid was leaving, and this time she had brought her gun. She felt its comforting weight in her under-arm holster as she sat questioning Kyander. He couldn't possibly know she was bluffing. "It's not every day that you send innocent men to certain death."

Kyander loosened his collar and worked his jaw as if it hurt. "Who did you say the man was?"

"A Soviet soldier who surrendered, was sent to Suursaari because he was Jewish, and then was transferred to Auschwitz. Now he's come over here." Hella leaned forward, forcing herself to meet Kyander's beady eyes above the whisky bottle from which he'd been drinking when she arrived. "And, in case you're wondering, he's in a safe place now, so the likes of you don't go looking for him." A lie, but how was he to know? Hella went on. "So that man, that soldier – his name's Yakov – he told me what happened to him, and to others like him. He gave me your name." She jammed her index finger into Kyander's chest. "You were a Nazi, a real one, you sent those people to a death camp, and I think my father knew something like that was going to happen, and he was trying to stop it. Is that why you killed my family?"

"I didn't kill them." Kyander shook his head. "True, there was a camp on Suursaari for the Jews we captured in the Soviet Union, and I heard that the Gestapo requested that some of these people be sent to Auschwitz. It was not my decision. I was just providing administrative assistance. Your father never really understood that. When he came to find me, he was practically incoherent. He said the Nazis had suggested we round up some Jews and send them to a concentration camp in Germany. When he refused the suggestion, they pushed him to resign. Your father wanted to go to the press and to the Interior Ministry, tell them what the Nazis planned for the Jews. I told him I'd talk to the Gestapo, calm things down. No one would get hurt. And that it was in his interest to be quiet about that. Especially given —"

"What?" Hella said. She wanted to kick him, to turn that fat glistening face into raw bloody pulp, like something coming out of her mother's meat grinder.

Kyander must have felt her fury. He shuffled uncomfortably. "His lineage."

"What?"

"Your name. Mauzer. Not really a Finnish name, etymologically speaking. Comes from Germany originally, doesn't it?"

"Yes," Hella said. She was livid with rage. "And in case you were wondering, it means vermin controller."

"How apt." Kyander shook his head. "Well, this whole country is a melting pot, anyway. My own name is Swedish in origin – I've even wondered from time to time whether I should Fennicize it as Kiianmies. But the point is, your father had a German name, and if the story about a SUPO agent handing over Jews to the Gestapo got out, everyone would have thought it was him. What you don't seem to understand is that I was trying to protect him. For his own good."

Hella didn't say anything. Her throat was paper-dry with rage.

"My dear child, you have to understand how things were at the time. Our government didn't really like the Nazis. They didn't want the Gestapo here, they didn't want to get involved, they even wanted to protect the Jews, only things didn't happen that way. No one's fault."

Hella's eyes blazed. "But it wasn't my father, it was *you* who was the real Nazi. No one forced you to collaborate with the Gestapo. You could have resigned as well. Did they ask you to kill my father to silence him?"

"Of course not." But Kyander's eyes were darting around the room now, looking for an escape. "The most I did was to try to smooth things over a little. But your father had his own way of seeing things, and frankly, it was becoming a nuisance. He was practically foaming at the mouth, told me we had to protect those Jews and that there was someone at the SUPO doing the Nazis' dirty work, informing and helping them. He said he was going to figure out who it was."

"You," Hella said. "It was you."

"You have no proof of that."

"I found the evidence that my father brought back with him from Suursaari," Hella said.

"It proves nothing at all!" Kyander threw his hands up in the air. "My dear child, how naive you are! A metal and barbed wire ashtray, what sort of proof is that? I knew you had it on your mantelpiece, I saw it when I came to gather his things. I suppose it's there still. But your father could have picked that up anywhere. You'll never be able to prove it was made by prisoners, that they gave it to him. I'll deny it absolutely. I'll say it's the most inept lie I've ever heard. You'll just make a fool of yourself, and that's all you'll ever achieve."

The ashtray, Hella thought, appalled. How many times had she looked at it over the last few days and never realized its significance? But Kyander had a point. She had no proof at all. Hella looked at the fat old man in front of her, his triple chin and his moist red lips, his white shirt straining against his stomach.

Oh yes, Kyander reeked of fear all right.

But he wasn't scared enough.

The small, shrewd eyes which now gazed back into hers were bright with menace. His hands were steady. And when he spoke again, his voice was belligerent.

"No one will believe you, ever. That Jewish man is certainly here illegally, and as you said yourself, he doesn't speak any Finnish. He's been gone too long. Who would believe him over me? And there's nothing to link me to your family's deaths. You can't prove that I've done anything."

She didn't need to think about it to know he was right. The ashtray on her mantelpiece meant nothing. And her visitor had supplied no proof of what he was advancing and had now disappeared again. But she also knew, knew with absolute certainty, that she would never find the truck driver. Not that he mattered much; he was just an instrument. Kyander had been behind all of it. Or possibly someone still higher up the chain of command, someone who had Nazi interests at heart, but all she had was Kyander. And no way to make him pay for what he'd done. As she stood there, facing him across six feet of plush carpet, her mind frantically seized on different options, which she discarded one by one.

Ask Steve to look into Kyander's past? He'd been dreaming about becoming an investigative reporter. But she knew Steve wouldn't find anything more, and certainly no proof that Kyander was involved.

What other options did she have? Should she kill him herself? Could she stare into those cold, pig-like eyes, take careful aim and pull the trigger?

As if reading her thoughts, Kyander said: "And don't you even think about taking justice into your own hands. Next time you come here, or someone comes on your behalf, I'll kill them. I'm getting old, my eyesight is poor, I'll pretend to have confused you for a burglar. They might not believe me, but as they'd see no reason why I'd want to kill the daughter of my oldest and closest friend, they'd let it slide. I'll be retired in a week. I won't even be a disgrace to the SUPO. And since you and Mustonen left, the homicide squad isn't what it once was. They'd dismiss it too."

And they probably would. She could imagine Kyander doing exactly that. *I'm heartbroken*, he would say. *You've got to believe me, officers. I would never have consciously hurt our dear little Hella. She surprised me. I acted on impulse.* And Inspector Pinchus would circle her body, tut-tutting, a gloomy smile on his face. Just like he had circled a different body the day before.

And suddenly, Hella had an idea.

42

In a way, Hella thought, it was the same old story but on a different scale. Just like Heikkinen had accused his mad cousin of killing his wife, so Kyander had pretended that her father would be accused of collaborating with the Nazis – and then killed him to cover his tracks. It was always the innocent who suffered. There was nothing new in that either.

Hella squinted into the orange glow of the sun as she made her way to Katajanokka. The streets were full of people in their Sunday best, the homes decorated with flowers and birch branches. When she was a child, her family always went to the countryside for Midsummer, building bonfires and staying up until dawn, the warm summer night filled with their singing voices. But tonight she was alone and there was a chill in the air. That was to be expected – Midsummer was a turning point, after all. Days were going to become short again. Darkness was coming.

She hoped she'd find Heikkinen at home. As she weaved her way through an increasingly drunk and excited crowd, Hella toyed with the idea of stopping at Headquarters, trying to see Jokela. She thought she knew what he'd say to her, though; she could almost hear his derisive snort – *My dear girl, what abuse are you talking about? A few slaps maybe, that's all* – and she kept on walking. She was repeating her lines as she walked, like an actor about to go on stage. Would he oblige her? She had no idea. That would almost certainly depend on whether he still considered her useful, whether he thought she had Jokela's ear.

On the corner of Kruunuvuorenkatu, Hella paused. A gaggle of laughing girls with flowers in their hair were blocking the passage. Hella wondered how they'd react if she told them she was going to a murderer's house. On a night like this, you were supposed to be celebrating with your loved ones. But hers had been taken from her a long time ago. Or, at the very least, you were supposed to be making bath whisks, stashing flower petals under your pillow and dreaming about your fiancé. One of the girls turned and smiled at her. "Where are your flowers?"

"I'm just about to get them," Hella muttered, inching past. She could see Heikkinen's house further down the street; the ground-floor windows were lit. She quickened her step until she was almost running. As if there was an urgency to lay the dead to rest. She seemed to be the only one who cared about them, and it somehow felt that this endless summer night was the only time she could avenge them.

There were no birch branches to frame Heikkinen's door, and no decorations visible through the windows. Hella pressed the bell and prepared for a wait, but the door opened almost at once. At first glance, Heikkinen still seemed the same – pulled together and smart – but now there was a vertical frown between his eyebrows and his eyes held a pained expression.

"What can I do for you, Miss Mauzer? I didn't expect the pleasure of your company tonight." Even though he was smiling, he looked as if he might close the door in her face.

Quickly, Hella said: "I've just been to see my friend Mr Räikkönen. We need to talk."

There was a pause. He caught her gaze and held it, and she wondered if he was weighing his options, trying to assess how much she knew and what leverage she had.

Then he stepped aside, and she edged her way into the apartment. After the warm clean air of the street, it smelled cold and stale and Hella thought that she could still detect the salty, metallic tang of Aalto's blood – but perhaps that was her imagination. In the middle of the living room, she stopped and turned. Heikkinen was watching her with his arms crossed, his eyes wary behind the hooded lids. He'd been drinking. There was a bottle of Stolichnaya on the side table, and a glass, three-quarters full, right next to it.

"So what did your friend Mr Räikkönen tell you?" He emphasized *friend*, perhaps implying that he knew what sort of friendship it was.

Hella ignored the unvoiced accusation. "Did I ever tell you he was the pathologist who carried out the autopsy on your wife?"

Heikkinen pulled up a chair and straddled it, his arms on top of the backrest. "You didn't. But he must have found nothing worth mentioning at the time, and I doubt he could say anything new now that five years have passed."

Hella looked at him. "I'm not going to ask you if you loved your wife. My question is, did your wife love you?"

"How would I know?" Heikkinen shrugged, then reached for his glass. "She certainly promised before the priest and her whole family to love and to comfort me until death do us part. Is that what you came here for? To try to find out if my wife loved me?" He took a swig and closed his eyes, briefly.

"I came here to ask you for a favour. But before I tell you what it is that I need, I first want to tell you something. Dr

Räikkönen had noted the presence of cuts and bruises on your wife's body. According to him, these had not occurred in the course of your heroic efforts to save her. And there's only one person who could have made them. You."

"And so you want to do what, dig up her body? Destroy my reputation, annihilate my career prospects, and all in the name of what? Justice? You'll never prove anything."

"I probably won't. But the rumour will follow you, always. And Jokela will never give you the job."

Heikkinen laughed, except that it sounded more like a bark. "If you really want to know, Miss Mauzer, Maria never forgave me for marrying her. I suppose she talked to her sister about our married life. And what did she talk about? Blows. That's all she ever remembered. She didn't remember my kisses, or the diamond brooch I bought her, or my hand holding hers through the agony of childbirth. No. Just blows. Bruises. Scars. It's all she could ever talk about. Because they left a mark on her body? But so does childbirth, and she never once regretted that, even though our baby didn't live." Heikkinen shook his head, his gaze lost in that not-too-distant past. Then, slowly, his long, sensitive fingers released their grip on the glass. He looked up at Hella and smiled. "Well, you know what, young lady? She deserved what she got. I would never have hit her if she was different, if she was grateful for what she had."

"I see. So she brought it on herself, is that it? And then you killed her." It was not a question, merely a statement of fact. "You'd been feeding your wife sleeping pills, and she figured it out and spoke to Veikko. He tried them on a neighbour's dog. Once you found out about that, you knew that you could murder your wife and get away with it. Better, even: you expected to pin it on your cousin. It was

203

very smart of you." She looked at him, sitting there before her, a murderer in a white, well-pressed shirt, a man who didn't seem to be troubled by remorse. "You see, when I learned that your wife died like she did, I suspected you immediately. But there was something that bothered me: you could have let the house burn down to the ground and you didn't. You carried her body out of the fire. This man can't possibly be a murderer, I thought. He's done everything to preserve the evidence. But of course I didn't realize at the time that you had a scapegoat."

"That's just one way of looking at things."

"Naturally. And I suppose you covered your tracks well when you invited your cousin to visit you in the middle of the night. What did you say to get him to come over? That accident on the stairs – that was perfectly staged. And the can of petrol was a nice touch. I fell for it completely."

Heikkinen grinned. "You're right, it was perfect. Now why don't you get down to business? You wanted to ask me something."

"I do." She watched him sip vodka from his glass while she tried to find the right words. "You need to understand that I'm not here to make trouble. I never even knew your wife. Her sister didn't hire me. But I do have a problem that I think you can help to put right without great inconvenience to yourself. And then... and then we can forget we ever had this conversation."

"Blackmail." Heikkinen was studying her, his gaze calculating and cold.

"Indeed."

He laughed. "I never thought you were the sort to blackmail anybody."

"I never thought you were the sort to kill anybody. Looks like we were both mistaken."

"So how can I trust your word that if I do what you ask me, you'll never mention this again?"

"Here," Hella said. She reached into her handbag. "I've typed up a report for Jokela, where I confirm that all rumours and anonymous letters concerning you are false. It's dated and signed. I'll give it to you once we're done tonight, so you can mail it to Jokela yourself."

"Can I read it?"

"Of course." She waited while he read. After a while, Heikkinen returned the letter to her and settled back in his chair, watching her from under hooded lids. "So what is it you want me to do?"

"It's simple. You told me you were in charge of internal affairs at the SUPO. I'd like you to go and see someone on my behalf." She paused, struggling to control her voice. "I believe that man killed my family. Tell him you're investigating his past. Threaten him. I want him confessing to murder. And then I'll decide what to do with him." She glanced at Heikkinen. "His name's Kyander, and he lives just around the corner from here."

43

It didn't take Heikkinen long to get ready. He disappeared briefly into his bedroom before returning in a suit and a tie.

"I know the man, actually. A sneaky bastard. I played cards with him and he cheated, so you're in luck. He's not someone I'd hesitate to crush."

Hella smiled. "Then it should be easy."

"I'm going in an unofficial capacity," Heikkinen said. "But he knows who I am, what my role is at the SUPO. He'll also know that I'm about to become the new head of the homicide squad." There he paused, watching Hella through narrowed eyes. "That part depends on you, of course."

"Of course." Hella nodded. She had drunk cup after cup of strong black coffee as she perfected her plan, and now her heart was thudding louder than the bell that chimed the hour. "You can tell him what you told me, that you knew and liked my father. That Kyander has a choice. Either he confesses to my family's murder, or he faces an inquiry into what he did during the war, and to those poor people."

"An impossible choice."

"Indeed." When Heikkinen turned to grab his hat, she sneaked a glance at her watch. Half past seven already. It had taken everything she had to convince Inspector Pinchus that waiting in the shadows on the street was going to be worth his while. And on Juhannus night, too.

Heikkinen was by the door now, ready to go out into the warm scented night and see Kyander. "Are you coming with me?" he asked.

Hella nodded. "I think I'd better. Though he might get angry if he sees me."

There were so many people on the pavement – all drunk, all cheerful – that they struggled to push through. As they walked, Hella glanced at Heikkinen, at the narrow line of his lips and his jaw jutting forward. It must have taken them less than five minutes to get to Kyander's place, but it felt like hours. Hella's feet were leaden with foreboding, her heart racing as she tried to look serene.

Heikkinen didn't stop his steady progression until they reached their destination and he paused on the porch, admiring the flower beds and the gleaming paintwork. Then he raised his hand to knock, lightly at first, as if he didn't really want to be heard, and then louder.

This time, no sour maid came to answer the door. Heikkinen knocked again. At last, there was a faint voice from somewhere deep inside the house: "Come in, it's open."

Heikkinen pushed the door. The hall was full of shadows, its black-and-white tiles like a chessboard, a stuffed boar's head gazing down on them malevolently. In front of them, a set of doors opened onto yet more darkness, but to the left Hella could see an arch and, beyond it, a circle of warm yellow light projected by a table lamp.

Kyander, fat and drunk on his after-dinner whisky, was sitting in a chair by the fireplace, his face in the shadows. Almost mechanically, Hella took notice of her surroundings. A carafe, three-quarters empty, and a tumbler, both on a side table. A newspaper folded in two on the arm of the chair. All the windows were closed, the heavy curtains drawn against the night sun. The big old house had accumulated heat during the day, and it seemed to radiate from the bulbous, overstuffed furniture, rising in waves from the carpet. Kyander didn't move when he saw them. If he hadn't invited them to come in, Hella would have assumed he was asleep.

Heikkinen pulled a chair towards him and sat down. "Let's not pretend this is a social call, shall we?" He sneaked a glance at Hella, who had remained standing. "I happen to know Miss Mauzer quite well, and before that, I knew and respected her father. I also believe in the importance of high standards of behaviour for all SUPO employees." He grinned, suddenly. "Whoever was it that said that publicity is the soul of justice? It is certainly true that we need to be accountable for our actions, always, and be capable of withstanding public scrutiny."

Kyander leaned forward. "And you had nothing better to do on Juhannus night than to come and tell me that?" His voice was casual, but the pulse at one of his temples had begun to beat visibly.

"That's correct," Heikkinen said, still smiling. "And it seems to me that this is as good a time as any to settle this amicably, before we're forced to resort to the full-blown unpleasantness that an official investigation of your actions during the last war could quickly turn into. I want you to write a confession, admitting that you murdered the Mauzer family. If you do that, we won't look into *why*."

"So you *are* serious?" Kyander arched his eyebrows and whistled through his teeth in mock surprise. He tilted his head at Hella. "Is she your mistress? I must admit I underestimated her. I didn't think any man could possibly be interested."

Heikkinen didn't answer and the silence stretched, interminable. It was so quiet, Hella could hear her own breathing, which was too rapid. She was feeling physically sick, her bowels twisted by an invisible hand, her stomach rising. Just like the day her family had died.

"So what do you want from me exactly?" Kyander got up and paced. The starch of his collar had gone limp, and his face was red and bloated. "I have sacrificed forty years of my life and two marriages to the secret service. I am retiring in a few days."

Heikkinen looked bored. "I told you already. I want a confession. Explain the role you played in the murder of this woman's family."

"A confession?" The grimace on Kyander's face signified that his tolerance was stretched just about to its limit. "And what good would it do? To anyone?"

"Let me be the judge of that," Heikkinen said. "Do you have a pen and paper here?"

Kyander took a deep breath and blew it out slowly, so that they could see just how much effort he was putting into remaining calm. He shook his head. "Arriving at my place, in the middle of the night, like *burglars*. Attempting to steal my life and reputation from me, and I'm supposed to sit and do nothing?" He grabbed the whisky carafe and drank from it, not bothering to fill his glass. His hands were shaking. When the carafe was empty, he set it down. He seemed unsure of what to do next.

Heikkinen glanced at his watch. "A confession, please." His voice was dry and full of contempt. "I haven't got all night."

"Is that a joke?" Kyander was now shaking in a fit of helpless laughter, wiping the tears streaming down his cheeks with the back of his hand. "All this because during the war I was doing my job, which involved liaising with the Gestapo? Oh, all right. You win." Still laughing, he shuffled over to his desk and started fumbling inside a drawer. "No, really. You come here, into my house… Don't tell me you haven't been warned."

This is it, Hella thought. He's reacting just like I expected him to. He's too drunk to do otherwise.

Her mouth was dry and her lips were so stiff that the words sounded cracked when she whispered to Heikkinen, "I think he might have a —"

She didn't get to finish her sentence. There was a loud click, like a branch snapping under her feet, and she found herself staring down the barrel of a gun.

"This is exactly what I'll say," Kyander commented conversationally. "I mistook you for burglars. I'll be so awfully sorry…"

Out of a corner of her eye, Hella saw Heikkinen tense and his hand glide down to his ankle.

Kyander was still talking. "Not an ideal way to leave the service, but it looks like I don't have much choice. They'll believe me. Wouldn't want to —"

Now, Hella thought. In her mind's eye she saw Tom, at the mortuary, and Pinchus, lurking in the shadows outside. She thought that if she died now, it wouldn't matter, because she would have avenged her family. The time stretched, interminable. She was conscious of the sharp animal stink of Heikkinen's fear, and of Kyander's swaying hand. The man was so drunk, he could scarcely take aim. He wouldn't shoot, she thought. He's just trying to scare us. Only a drunk could think he'd get away with it. This is ridiculous. And Heikkinen, is he really planning to act like a cowboy? It certainly seemed like that, but then he was drunk too. Drunk and angry.

"Mr Kyander," she said. "Put down that gun and start writing your confession. And then we'll —"

The world around her exploded with sound and fury. She watched it in slow motion, as if she was far, far away, maybe where she had left her family all those years ago. Kyander taking a step back to absorb the recoil, and Heikkinen's taut, self-absorbed face, his raised arm. And then not even that. As she started falling, all she could see were the orange headlights of a truck, while the roar in her ears became that of an engine revving.

44

"I can't find the salt," Steve said. "It was in that little pot on the shelf above the stove last time I cooked, but it's not there any more." Then he paused. "Are you OK?" It was a bright summer morning and Steve was in her kitchen, cooking lunch, her mother's striped apron tied around his waist.

Hella dragged a hand across her eyes to brush away tears and sniffed. Could you salt meatballs with tears? And why not? You could have different flavours. *Broken-hearted. Lonely. Angry.* Or, like in the present case, *I-don't-know-why-I'm-crying* tears. She sniffed again. "No idea where it could be. Let's just do without."

"Now that's the most…" Smiling, Steve turned to face her, then paused. When he finally spoke, his voice had grown serious. "You're thinking about last night again. But that was a success, wasn't it? Given the circumstances?"

She said quietly. "A man died. That's not exactly what I would call a success."

"An evil man."

"Yes." If she closed her eyes, she could still see the blood blooming on the carpet like some exotic flower, and Inspector Pinchus' hunched form circling the body. This time around, he hadn't said that he found her presence suspicious, but she could still see him thinking just that. Every once in a while, Pinchus had stopped and peered at her, his eyes round with astonishment.

And now Steve was looking at her with the same expression. "Hella, they were both evil. As bad as they come. You knew that for sure about Heikkinen. As for Kyander… you've seen the file."

That file was the first thing she'd seen when she woke up. It had been delivered by a messenger, together with a note penned in Jokela's hand.

It looks like I did it again, the note said. *Please believe me when I tell you I didn't expect to put you in danger. Anyway, I'm sorry. You can have the file. You'll see that there's nothing in there that you haven't already discovered by yourself.*

Steve was still looking at her. "You shouldn't blame yourself. Tell me, did Pinchus get to make an arrest after all?"

She nodded. Something sharp was jammed in her side, and she lifted the sofa cushion to see what it was. A bouquet that Liisa Vanhanen had given her the other day, now wilted and losing petals. She had forgotten all about her Juhannus spells, not that it mattered – there were more important things than finding a husband. Such as finding a way to jail a murderer for life. Avenging her parents, and the Jewish refugees sent to die in a concentration camp. Turning a page.

Steve was still talking. "And so Heikkinen gets off for killing his wife and cousin but goes down for killing the man who caused the deaths of your entire family?"

She nodded again, a lump in her throat. "I so wanted to get justice for poor Maria, and for Veikko, too, but there was no proof. And this way, Heikkinen is behind bars for good. He came to Kyander's home without an invitation, he was armed, and he shot first. For Pinchus, that was all that mattered. As for me…"

"Yes?" Steve said.

Hella bit her lip, thinking. She had imagined it happening for so long, it had become a part of her: the moment she made the arrest, or pulled the trigger, or otherwise cleared the earth of the vermin that had killed her family. It had always been at the back of her mind, ever since she was eighteen, but now that it was over she felt empty. Nauseous. She didn't want to talk about it, but Steve was waiting for something, and so she said: "I'm glad Kyander is dead."

"Of course you are." Steve gave one final stir to the meatballs in the pan. "Where's your plate? The food's ready."

"I'm not hungry," Hella said. She wondered if she'd ever eat again. Or sleep again. Or manage to think of something else but the dead body on the floor.

Steve put the pan down and sighed. He wiped his hands on the apron and reached into his back pocket. "Then I did well not to put it inside a meatball. That was my first idea. Luckily, I changed my mind." The expression on his face was part grin, part embarrassment. He waited until she met his gaze. "By the way, your handsome neighbour came by this morning, while you were upstairs. I told him to get lost." Steve arched an eyebrow, but she could see panic in his eyes too. "I hope you don't mind."

"I don't."

"Well, then."

Hella watched in disbelief as he got down on his knees and held open a small box. A smile twinkled sheepishly across his face, and in the morning sunlight his hair and lashes gleamed gold. Same as the ring inside the box.

Hella blinked. "What are you, mad?" She wondered briefly whether her mind was playing tricks on her. Maybe *she* was the one who was going mad? That wouldn't be much of a surprise. She glanced down at the wilted bouquet lying on a sofa cushion next to her. She was delusional. She needed coffee, to stay sharp. Not meatballs.

"Hella Mauzer, will you marry me?"

She thought of all the sleepless nights she'd spent waiting for him, of all the years and months and days she hadn't dared hope that he'd ever propose. And now this. Out of the blue.

"Why?"

"You're a good cook."

Hella snorted, a bubble of laughter rising in her throat, like champagne.

"You know how to keep house." A smile was tugging at the corners of Steve's mouth as he tried not to glance at the mayhem around him. "You are a little woman who cannot survive without a man in her life."

She thought of hitting him with the bouquet, but there was something she needed to tell him first, before things got out of hand.

"Get up, Steve, please. And close that box. We need to talk."

His lips narrowed but he did as he was told, pulling a chair towards him and sitting down heavily. His hands were clasped around the box.

There was no good way to say it. She just had to get on with it. "I've been feeling unwell lately." That was an understatement, but Steve didn't need to know the details. "I thought at first it was the aftermath of my accident, or maybe food poisoning." She shrugged. "Or just that I was getting old. But it's not that."

"What is it then? Have you seen a doctor?"

"I was wondering if you'd noticed anything. If that was the reason you proposed."

"What kind of reason?" He caught her gaze and held it. "What do you mean?"

"I'm pregnant, Steve. Four months, it must be. Before the accident, when you and I, when we…" She choked on the words. "Tom told me that the accident's not a problem, that it should be all right, because apparently the placenta is one of the first-priority organs." She took a deep breath. "I don't want you to marry me just because of the baby."

"But I'm not…" Steve looked gobsmacked. "Hella, this is wonderful. A baby! I didn't even imagine." He was looking at her like she was the most precious thing in the world. Then, slowly, he slid back to his knees again. "Hella Mauzer, will you marry me? Not because of your cooking or your housekeeping skills, or your maternal instincts, though it would be fun to see those. But because I love you." He opened the box again. She looked at the ring, but she couldn't really see it. All she saw were his hands, and they were shaking.

She took a deep breath. Why was this so hard? She knew what she wanted. She also knew that no one would understand. She could hardly understand it herself. *Stubborn as a donkey*, they would say. *Different. How can she ever be a good mother?* But she was as she was, and it was too late to change. Besides, she didn't want to. She was used to making her own decisions, being accountable to no one.

"I'm having your child, Steve," she said. "I've decided to keep it, though I wasn't sure at first. But I won't marry you. I can't be a perfect little housewife, frying meatballs and mending socks. And I can't be dependent on you." He started to say something, and she silenced him with a raised hand. "So I want to keep on working." She shrugged. "Maybe I'm not the marrying type, or maybe I'll regret it. But the thing is, you could still try to be a parent. We could be parents together. You and I. We just have to find a way to make that work."

There was a long silence; it seemed to her that they were both holding their breath. Then, slowly, Steve closed the box and put away the ring.

Hella smiled. She could imagine herself walking down a Helsinki street, pushing a stroller, ringless, alone. An unwed mother who was also a private investigator. An outcast.

And that was fine. It really was.

Acknowledgements

I am beholden to my editor, François von Hurter, for his insights and superb guidance during the writing of this book. Thank you also to Laurence Colchester, for being such a pleasure to work with.

Much thanks to my agent, Marilia Savvides of 42, for her unwavering confidence in me and her enthusiasm, and to Alexandra Kordas, also of 42, for introducing Miss Mauzer to Hollywood. Fingers crossed she'd like it there.

More thanks to my brilliant copy-editor, Sarah Terry – she is the absolute best, and I don't say it lightly.

For his expertise in fields of which I knew nothing and for explaining it all to me in plain English, thanks to Mark Billington.

A precious source of information on 1950s Finland was Diana Webster's autobiographical book *Finland Forevermore* – an engrossing and well-documented read that I highly recommend for those interested in that time and place. I am also indebted to the Chabad Lubavitch of Finland, which published a vivid account of the fate of Jewish refugees and prisoners of war, including descriptions of conditions in the Suursaari camp and the true story of eight Jewish prisoners who had been betrayed by a high-ranking Finnish state police official and handed over to the Gestapo, which sent them to die in Auschwitz. This account is further confirmed in Oula Silvennoinen's article 'Helsinki: On the Brink – Finland and the Holocaust Era', which appears in the anthology *Civil Society and the Holocaust: International Perspectives on Resistance and Rescue.* That being said, I hope that my readers will forgive me for taking some liberties with historical facts. Please remember that this novel is fiction and is not based on real events. The Mauzer family never existed – though I've spent so much time with them, it sometimes feels to me as if they did.

Finally, much love and appreciation to my husband – who I'm happy to report was *not* an inspiration for the characters in this book – and to my children, for being such fun to be around. I love you all.